DON QUIXOTE
OF THE MANCHA

DON QUIXOTE
TESTING HIS HELMET

·DON·QVIXOTE· OF·THE·MANCHA·

RETOLD·
BY·
JUDGE·
PARRY.

ILLUSTRA
TED·BY
WALTER·
CRANE.

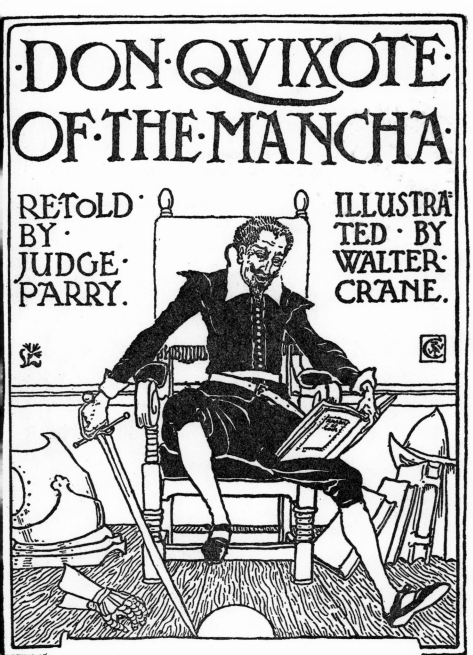

DODD, MEAD AND CO.
NEW YORK   1960

Published 1954
by Dodd, Mead & Company, Inc.

PREFACE

A VERSION of *Don Quixote* which is appended to Mr. Walter Crane's illustrations needs perhaps no apology, but I desire to state briefly what I have endeavoured to do. No existing abridgment of *Don Quixote,* known to me, gives in simple narrative form the adventures of Knight and Squire, with as much of the wisdom and humour of their discourse as would be within the grasp of the younger generation of readers. This—*The Story of Don Quixote,* as I call it—I have tried to produce. In doing it I have made use of all the English translations, but the basis of this book is Thomas Shelton's translation, the language of which seems to me better to express the humour of Cervantes than any other. Many will consider such a task in the nature of sacrilege or, at the best, verging on the impertinent. With these views I have much sympathy myself. But at least, let it be understood that all I have attempted to do is to tell a well-known story in print, as one who loves it would seek to tell it in words, to those around his own fireside; in the hope that some may gather from this story that there is a vast storehouse of humour and wisdom awaiting them in the book itself.

CONTENTS

LIST OF ILLUSTRATIONS

FULL PAGES

HALF PAGES

DON QUIXOTE
OF THE MANCHA

CHAPTER I

An Introduction to that famous gentleman,

Don Quixote of the Mancha

THIS is the story that Miguel de Cervantes, Spaniard, published in 1605, which the world has been reading again and again ever since.

Once upon a time there lived in a certain village in a province of Spain called the Mancha, a gentleman named Quixada or Queseda—for indeed historians differ about this—whose house was full of old lances, halberds, and such other armours and weapons. He was, besides, the owner of an ancient target or shield, a raw-boned steed, and a swift greyhound. His pot consisted daily of common meats, some lentils on Fridays, and perhaps a roast pigeon for Sunday's dinner. His dress was a black suit with velvet britches, and slippers of the same colour, which he kept for holidays, and a suit of homespun which he wore on week-days.

On the purchase of these few things he spent the small rents that came to him every year. He had in his house a woman-servant of about some forty years old, a Niece not yet twenty, and a lad that served him both in field and at home, and could saddle his horse or manage a pruning-hook.

The master himself was about fifty years old, a strong, hard-featured man with a withered face. He was an early riser, and had once been very fond of hunting. But now for a great portion of the year he applied himself wholly to reading the old books of Knighthood, and this with such keen delight that he forgot all about the pleasures of the chase, and neglected all household matters. His mania and folly grew to such a pitch that he sold many acres of his lands to buy books of the exploits and adventures of the Knights of old. These he took for true and correct histories, and when his friends the Curate of the village, or Mr. Nicholas, the worthy Barber of the town, came to see him, he would dispute with them as to which of the Knights of romance had done the greatest deeds.

So eagerly did he plunge into the reading of these books that he many times spent whole days and nights poring over them; and in the end, through little sleep and much reading, his brain became tired, and he fairly lost his wits. His fancy was filled with those things that he read, of enchantments, quarrels, battles, challenges, wounds, wooings, loves, tempests, and other impossible follies, and those romantic tales so firmly took hold of him that he believed no history to be so certain and sincere as they were.

Finally, his wit being extinguished, he was seized with one of the strangest whims that ever madman stumbled on in this world, for it seemed to him right and necessary that he himself should become a Knight Errant, and ride through the world in arms to seek adventures and practise in person all that he had read about the Knights of old. Therefore he resolved that he would make a name for himself by revenging the injuries of others, and courting all manner of dangers and difficulties, until in the end he should be rewarded for his valour in arms by the crown of some mighty Empire. And first of all he caused certain old rusty arms that belonged to his great-grandfather, and had lain for many years neglected and forgotten in a by-corner of his house, to be brought out and well scoured. He trimmed them and dressed them as well as he could, and then saw that they had something wanting, for instead of a proper helmet they had only a morion or headpiece, like a steel bonnet without any visor. This his industry supplied, for he made a visor for his helmet by patching and pasting certain papers together, and this pasteboard fitted to the morion gave it all the appearance of a real helmet. Then, to make sure that it was strong enough, he out with his sword and gave it a blow or two, and with the very first did quite undo that which had cost him a week to make. He did not at all approve the ease with which it was destroyed, and to make things better he placed certain iron bars within it, in such a manner that made him feel sure it was now sound and strong, without putting it to a second trial.

He next visited his horse, who though he had more corners than a Spanish *real* or shilling, which in those days was anything but round, and had nothing on him but skin and bone, yet he seemed to him a better steed than Bucephalus, the noble animal that carried Alexander the Great when he went to battle. He spent four days inventing a name for his horse, saying to himself that it was not fit that so famous a Knight's horse, and so good a beast, should want a known name. Therefore he tried to find a name that should both give people some notion of what he had been before he was the steed of a Knight Errant, and also what he now was; for, seeing that his lord and master was going to change his calling, it was only right that his horse should have a new name, famous and high-sounding, and worthy of his new position in life. And after having chosen, made up, put aside, and thrown over any number of names as not coming up to his idea, he finally hit upon Rozinante, a name in his opinion sublime and well-sounding, expressing in a word what he had been when he was a simple carriage horse, and what was expected of him in his new dignity.

The name being thus given to his horse, he made up his mind to give himself a name also, and in that thought laboured another eight days. Finally he determined to call himself Don Quixote, which has made people think that his name was Quixada and not Queseda, as others have said; and remembering that the great Knights of olden time were not satisfied with a mere dry name, but added to it the name of their kingdom or country, so he like a good Knight added to his own that also of his province, and called himself Don Quixote of the Mancha, whereby he declared his birthplace and did honour to his country by taking it for his surname.

His armour being scoured, his morion transformed into

a helmet, his horse named, and himself furnished with a new name, he considered that now he wanted nothing but a lady on whom he might bestow his service and affection. 'For,' he said to himself, remembering what he had read in the books of knightly adventures, 'if I should by good hap encounter with some Giant, as Knights Errant ordinarily do, and if I should overthrow him with one blow to the ground, or cut him with a stroke in two halves, or finally overcome and make him yield to me, it would be only right and proper that I should have some lady to whom I might present him. Then would he, entering my sweet lady's presence, say unto her with a humble and submissive voice: "Madam, I am the Giant Caraculiambro, Lord of the Island called Malindrania, whom the never-too-much-praised Knight Don Quixote of the Mancha hath overcome in single combat. He hath commanded me to present myself to your greatness, that it may please your Highness to dispose of me according to your liking."'

You may believe that the heart of the Knight danced for joy when he made that grand speech, and he was even more pleased when he had found out one whom he might call his lady. For, they say, there lived in the next village to his own a hale, buxom country wench with whom he was sometime in love, though for the matter of that she had never known of it or taken any notice of him whatever. She was called Aldonca Lorenso, and her he thought fittest to honour as the lady of his fancy. Then he began to search about in his mind for a name that should not vary too much from her own, but should at the same time show people that she was a Princess or lady of quality. Thus it was that he called her Dulcinea of Toboso, a name sufficiently strange, romantic, and musical for the lady of so brave a Knight. And now, having taken to himself both armour, horse, and lady fair, he was ready to go forth and seek adventures.

DON·QUIXOTE·WATCHING·HIS·ARMOUR·

CHAPTER II

Of the First Sally that Don Quixote made to

seek Adventures

ALL his preparations being made, he could no longer resist the desire of carrying out his plans, his head being
full of the wrongs he intended to put right, the errors he
wished to amend, and the evil deeds he felt himself
called upon to punish. And, therefore, without telling
any living creature, and unseen of anybody, somewhat
before daybreak—it being one of the warmest days in
July—he armed himself from head to foot, mounted on
Rozinante, laced on his strange helmet, gathered up his
target, seized his lance, and through the back door of his
yard sallied forth into the fields, marvellously cheerful

and content to see how easily he had started on his new career. But scarcely was he clear of the village when he was struck by a terrible thought, and one which did well-nigh overthrow all his plans. For he recollected that he had never been knighted, and therefore, according to the laws of Knighthood, neither could he nor ought he to combat with any Knight. And even if he were a Knight, he remembered to have read that as a new Knight he ought to wear white armour without any device upon his shield until he should win it by force of arms.

These thoughts made him waver a little in his plan; but more the reason that his head was full of his folly than for any other, he determined to cause himself to be knighted by the first he met, as others had done of whom he had read in the books which had so turned his brain. As to the white armour, he resolved at the first opportunity to scour his own until it should be whiter than ermine; and, having satisfied himself with these intentions, he pursued his way without following any other road than that which his horse was pleased to choose, believing that to be the most correct way of meeting with knightly adventures. And as he rode along he exclaimed to the empty air as if he had been actually in love: 'O Princess Dulcinea, Lady of this captive heart, much wrong hast thou done me by dismissing me and reproaching me with thy cruel commandment not to appear before thy beauty! I pray thee, sweet Lady, to remember this thy faithful slave, who for thy love suffers so many tortures.'

A thousand other ravings, after the style and manner that his books had taught him, did he add to this as he travelled along, meeting with no adventure worthy to be set down, whilst the sun mounted so swiftly and with so great heat that it would have been sufficient to have melted his brains if he had had any left.

He journeyed all that day long, and at night both he and his horse were tired and marvellously pressed by hunger, and looking about him on every side to see whether he could discover any Castle to which he might retire for the night, he saw an Inn near unto the highway on which he travelled, which was as welcome a sight to him as if he had seen a guiding star. Then spurring his horse he rode towards it as fast as he might, and arrived there much about nightfall.

There stood by chance at the Inn door two jolly peasant women who were travelling towards Seville with some carriers, who happened to take up their lodging in that Inn the same evening. And as our Knight Errant believed all that he saw or heard to take place in the same manner as he had read in his books, he no sooner saw the Inn than he fancied it to be a Castle with four turrets and pinnacles of shining silver, with a drawbridge, a deep moat, and all such things as belong to grand Castles. Drawing slowly towards it, he checked Rozinante with the bridle when he was close to the Inn, and rested awhile to see if any dwarf would mount on the battlements to give warning with the sound of a trumpet how some Knight did approach the Castle; but seeing they stayed so long, and Rozinante was eager to get up to his

stable, he went to the Inn door, and there beheld the two
wenches that stood at it, whom he supposed to be two
beautiful damsels or lovely ladies that did solace themselves before the Castle gates. At that moment it happened that a certain swineherd, as he gathered together
his hogs, blew the horn which was wont to bring them
together, and at once Don Quixote imagined it was some
dwarf who gave notice of his arrival; and he rode up to
the Inn door with marvellous delight. The ladies, when
they beheld one armed in that manner with lance and
target, made haste to run into the Inn; but Don Quixote,
seeing their fear by their flight, lifted up his pasteboard
visor, showed his withered and dusky face, and spoke to
them thus: 'Let not your ladyships fly nor fear any harm,
for it does not belong to the order of Knighthood which
I profess to wrong anybody, much less such high-born
damsels as your appearance shows you to be.'

The wenches looked at him very earnestly, and sought
with their eyes for his face, which the ill-fashioned helmet concealed; but when they heard themselves called
high-born damsels, they could not contain their laughter,
which was so loud that Don Quixote was quite ashamed
of them and rebuked them, saying: 'Modesty is a comely
ornament of the beautiful, and too much laughter spring-
ing from trifles is great folly; but I do not tell you this to
make you the more ashamed, for my desire is none other
than to do you all the honour and service I may.'

This speech merely increased their laughter, and with
it his anger, which would have passed all bounds if the
Innkeeper had not come out at this instant. Now this

Innkeeper was a man of exceeding fatness, and therefore, as some think, of a very peaceable disposition; and when he saw that strange figure, armed in such fantastic armour, he was very nearly keeping the two women company in their merriment and laughter. But being afraid of the owner of such a lance and target, he resolved to behave civilly for fear of what might happen, and thus addressed him: 'Sir Knight! if your Worship do seek for lodging, we have no bed at liberty, but you shall find all other things in abundance.'

To which Don Quixote, noting the humility of the Constable of the Castle—for such he took him to be—replied: 'Anything, Sir Constable, may serve me, for my arms are my dress, and the battlefield is my bed.'

While he was speaking, the Innkeeper laid hand on Don Quixote's stirrup and helped him to alight. This he did with great difficulty and pain, for he had not eaten a crumb all that day. He then bade the Innkeeper have special care of his horse, saying he was one of the best animals that ever ate bread.

The Innkeeper looked at Rozinante again and again, but he did not seem to him half so good as Don Quixote valued him. However, he led him civilly to the stable, and returned to find his guest in the hands of the high-born damsels, who were helping him off with his armour. They had taken off his back and breast plates, but they could in no way get his head and neck out of the strange, ill-fashioned helmet which he had fastened on with green ribands.

Now these knots were so impossible to untie that the

wenches would have cut them, but this Don Quixote would not agree to. Therefore he remained all the night with his helmet on, and looked the drollest and strangest figure you could imagine. And he was now so pleased with the women, whom he still took to be ladies and dames of the Castle, that he said to them: 'Never was Knight so well attended on and served by ladies as was Don Quixote. When he departed from his village, damsels attended on him and princesses on his horse. O ladies! Rozinante is the name of my steed, and I am called Don Quixote, and the time shall come when your ladyships may command me and I obey, and then the valour of mine arm shall discover the desire I have to do you service.'

The women could make nothing of this talk, but asked him if he would eat, and Don Quixote replying that such was his desire, there was straightway laid a table at the Inn door. The Host brought out a portion of badly boiled haddocks, and a black, greasy loaf, which was all the Inn could supply. But the manner of Don Quixote's eating was the best sport in the world, for with his helmet on he could put nothing into his mouth himself if others did not help him to find his way, and therefore one of the wenches served his turn at that, and helped to feed him. But they could not give him drink after that manner, and he would have remained dry for ever if the Innkeeper had not bored a cane, and putting one end in his mouth, poured the wine down the other. And all this he suffered rather than cut the ribands of his helmet.

And as he sat at supper the swineherd again sounded

his horn, and Don Quixote was still firm in the belief that he was in some famous Castle where he was served with music, and that the stale haddock was fresh trout, the bread of the finest flour, the two wenches high-born damsels, and the Innkeeper the Constable of the Castle. Thus he thought his career of Knight Errant was well begun, but he was still greatly troubled by the thought that he was not yet dubbed Knight, and could not therefore rightly follow his adventures until he received the honour of Knighthood.

CHAPTER III

Of the Pleasant Manner of the Knighting of
Don Quixote

WHEN he had finished his sorry supper, he took his host with him to the stable, and shutting the door threw himself down upon his knees before him, saying: 'I will never rise from this place where I am, Sir Constable, until your courtesy shall grant me a boon that I mean to demand of you, something which will add to your renown and to the profit of all the human race.'

The Innkeeper, seeing his guest at his feet, and hearing him speak these words, stood confounded at the sight, not knowing what he would say or do next, and tried to make him arise. But all was in vain until he had promised him that he would grant him any gift that he sought at his hands.

'Signor,' said Don Quixote, rising from his knees, 'I did never expect less from your great magnificence, and now I will tell you that the boon which I demand of you, and which you have so generously granted, is that to-morrow in the morning you will dub me Knight. This night I will watch mine armour in the Chapel of your Castle, and in the morning, as I have said, the rest of my desires shall be fulfilled, that I may set out in a proper manner

THE KNIGHTING OF
DON QUIXOTE

throughout the four parts of the world to seek adventures to the benefit of the poor and needy, as is the duty of Knighthood and of Knights Errant.'

The Innkeeper, who was a bit of a jester, and had before thought that the wits of his guest were none of the best, was sure that his suspicions were true when he heard him speak in this manner. And in order to enjoy a joke at his expense, he resolved to fall in with his humour, and told him that there was great reason in what he desired, which was only natural and proper in a Knight of such worth as he seemed to be. He added further that there was no Chapel in his Castle where he might watch his arms, for he had broken it down to build it up anew. But, nevertheless, he knew well that in a case of necessity they might be watched in any other place, and therefore he might watch them that night in the lower court of the Castle, where in the morning he, the Innkeeper, would perform all the proper ceremonies, so that he should be made not only a dubbed Knight, but such a one as should not have a fellow in the whole universe.

The Innkeeper now gave orders that Don Quixote should watch his armour in a great yard that lay near unto one side of the Inn, wherefore he gathered together all his arms, laid them on a cistern near to a well, and buckling on his target he laid hold of his lance and walked up and down before the cistern very demurely, until night came down upon the scene.

In the meantime the roguish Innkeeper told all the rest that lodged in the Inn of the folly of his guest, the

watching of his arms, and the Knighthood which he expected to receive. They all wondered very much at so
strange a kind of folly, and going out to behold him from
a distance, they saw that sometimes he marched to and
fro with a quiet gesture, other times leaning upon his
lance he looked upon his armour for a good space of
time without beholding any other thing save his arms.

Although it was now night, yet was the moon so clear
that everything which the Knight did was easily seen by
all beholders. And now one of the carriers that lodged
in the Inn resolved to give his mules some water, and for
that purpose it was necessary to move Don Quixote's
armour that lay on the cistern.

Seeing the carrier approach, Don Quixote called to
him in a loud voice: 'O thou, whosoever thou art, bold
Knight, who dares to touch the armour of the bravest
adventurer that ever girded sword, look well what thou
doest, and touch them not if thou meanest not to leave
thy life in payment for thy meddling!'

The carrier took no notice of these words, though it
were better for him if he had, but laying hold of the armour threw it piece by piece into the middle of the yard.

When Don Quixote saw this, he lifted up his eyes
towards heaven, and addressing his thoughts, as it
seemed, to his Lady Dulcinea, he said: 'Assist me, dear
Lady, in this insult offered to thy vassal, and let not thy
favour and protection fail me in this my first adventure!'

Uttering these and other such words, he let slip his
target or shield, and lifting up his lance with both hands
he gave the carrier so round a knock on his pate that it

overthrew him on to the ground, and if he had caught him a second he would not have needed any surgeon to cure him. This done, he gathered up his armour again, and laying the pieces where they had been before, he began walking up and down near them with as much quietness as he did at first.

But very soon afterwards another carrier, without knowing what had happened, for his companion yet lay on the ground, came also to give his mules water, and coming to take away the armour to get at the cistern, Don Quixote let slip again his target, and lifting his lance brought it down on the carrier's head, which he broke in several places.

All the people in the Inn, and amongst them the Innkeeper, came running out when they heard the noise, and Don Quixote seeing them seized his target, and, drawing his sword, cried aloud: 'O Lady of all beauty, now, if ever, is the time for thee to turn the eyes of thy greatness on thy Captive Knight who is on the eve of so marvellous great an adventure.'

Saying this seemed to fill him with so great a courage, that if he had been assaulted by all the carriers in the universe he would not have retreated one step.

The companions of the wounded men, seeing their fellows in so evil a plight, began to rain stones on Don Quixote from a distance, who defended himself as well as he might with his target, and durst not leave the cistern lest he should appear to abandon his arms.

The Innkeeper cried to them to let him alone, for he had already told them that he was mad. But all the time

Don Quixote cried out louder than the Innkeeper, calling them all disloyal men and traitors, and that the Lord of the Castle was a treacherous and bad Knight to allow them to use a Knight Errant so basely; and if he had only received the order of Knighthood he would have punished him soundly for his treason. Then calling to the carriers he said: 'As for you base and rascally ruffians, you are beneath my notice. Throw at me, approach, draw near and do me all the hurt you may, for you shall ere long receive the reward of your insolence.'

These words, which he spoke with great spirit and boldness, struck a terrible fear into all those who assaulted him, and, partly moved by his threats and partly persuaded by the Innkeeper, they left off throwing stones at him, and he allowed them to carry away the wounded men, while he returned to his watch with great quietness and gravity.

The Innkeeper did not very much like Don Quixote's pranks, and therefore determined to shorten the ceremony and give him the order of Knighthood at once before anyone else was injured. Approaching him, therefore, he made apologies for the insolence of the base fellows who had thrown stones at him, and explained that it was not with his consent, and that he thought them well punished for their impudence. He added that it was not necessary for Don Quixote to watch his armour any more, because the chief point of being knighted was to receive the stroke of the sword on the neck and shoulder, and that ceremony he was ready to perform at once.

All this Don Quixote readily believed, and answered

that he was most eager to obey him, and requested him to finish everything as speedily as possible. For, he said, as soon as he was knighted, if he was assaulted again, he intended not to leave one person alive in all the Castle, except those which the Constable should command, whom he would spare for his sake.

The Innkeeper, alarmed at what he said, and fearing lest he should carry out his threat, set about the ceremony without delay. He brought out his day-book, in which he wrote down the accounts of the hay and straw which he sold to carriers who came to the Inn, and attended by a small boy holding the end of a candle and walking before him, and followed by the two women who were staying at the Inn, he approached Don Quixote. He solemnly commanded him to kneel upon his knees, while he mumbled something which he pretended to read out of the book that he held in his hand. Then he gave him a good blow on the neck, and after that another sound thwack over the shoulders with his own sword, always as he did so continuing to mumble and murmur as though he were reading something out of his book. This being done, he commanded one of the damsels to gird on his sword, which she did with much grace and cleverness. And it was with difficulty that they all kept from laughing during this absurd ceremony, but what they had already seen of Don Quixote's fury made them careful not to annoy him even by a smile.

When she had girded on his sword, the damsel said: 'May you be a fortunate Knight, and meet with good success in all your adventures.'

Don Quixote asked her how she was called, that he might know to whom he was obliged for the favours he had received. She answered with great humility that she was named Tolosa, and was a butcher's daughter of Toledo. Don Quixote replied requesting her to call herself from henceforth the Lady Tolosa, which she promised to perform. The other damsel buckled on his spurs, and when Don Quixote asked her name she told him it was Molinera, and that she was daughter of an honest miller of Antequera. Don Quixote entreated her also to call herself Lady Molinera, and offered her new services and favours.

These strange and never-to-be-seen ceremonies being ended, Don Quixote could not rest until he was mounted on horseback that he might go to seek adventures. He therefore caused Rozinante to be instantly saddled, leaped on his back, and embracing the Innkeeper, thanked him in a thousand wild and ridiculous ways for the great favour he had done him in dubbing him Knight. The Innkeeper, who was only eager to be rid of him without delay, answered him in the same fashion, and let him march off without demanding from him a single farthing for his food and lodging.

DON·QUIXOTE·
·TO·THE·RESCUE·
OF·ANDREW·

CHAPTER IV

Of what befell our Knight when he left
the Inn

IT was dawn when Don Quixote went out from the Inn,
so full of pleasure to behold himself knighted that his
very horse-girths were ready to burst for joy. But calling
to memory some advice that the Innkeeper had given
him, about the necessity of carrying with him money
and clean shirts when he went on his adventures, he
determined to return to his house and obtain these
things, and also find for himself a Squire. For this office
he fixed in his own mind upon a ploughman, a neighbour
of his, a poor man who had many children, but yet a man
who was very fit as he thought to be his Squire.

With this view he turned Rozinante towards his own

21

village, who, knowing that he was on his way home, began to trot along with so good a will that he seemed not to touch the ground.

He had not travelled far when he heard from a thicket hard by the shrill cries of some weak and delicate mortal in grievous distress.

No sooner did he hear them than he exclaimed: 'I am indeed thankful for the favour done to me by giving me so soon an opportunity of performing what is due to my profession, and gathering the fruits of my desires. These cries doubtless come from some distressed man or woman who has need of my protection and aid.'

Then turning the reins, he guided Rozinante towards the place whence the voice seemed to proceed. And within a few paces after he had entered into the thicket, he saw a mare tied up to one oak, and to another was tied a youth, all naked from the middle upward, of about fifteen years of age. Now it was he that cried so pitifully, and not without cause. For a sturdy fellow of a farmer was beating him soundly with a girdle, accompanying each stroke with a reproof and piece of advice, saying: 'The tongue must peace and the eyes be wary.' And the boy, whose name was Andrew, answered: 'I will never do it again, good master, I will never do it again. I promise to have more care of your things from henceforth.'

Seeing what passed, Don Quixote cried out with an angry voice: 'Ill it beseems you, discourteous Knight, to deal thus with one that cannot defend himself. Mount, therefore, on horseback and take thy lance (for the Farmer had a lance leaning against the very same tree

to which his mare was tied), for I will make thee know
that it is the act of a coward to do that which thou dost.'

The Farmer, beholding this strange figure buckled in
armour, and brandishing a lance over his head, gave
himself up for a dead man, and answered him with mild
and submissive words, saying: 'Sir Knight, the youth
whom I am beating is mine own servant, and keepeth
for me a flock of sheep; but he is grown so negligent that
he loseth one of them every other day, and because I
correct him for his carelessness and knavery, he says I
do it through covetousness and miserliness so as not to
pay him his due wages, but on my conscience I assure·
you he lies.'

'What? The lie, in my presence, rascally clown!' cried
Don Quixote. 'By the sun that shines above us, I will
run thee through and through with my lance, base Carle!
Pay him instantly, without another word, or I will finish
and destroy thee in a moment. Loose him forthwith!'

The Farmer, hanging down his head, made no reply,
but released poor Andrew, of whom Don Quixote demanded how much his master owed him. The boy answered that it was nine months' wages at seven *reals* a
month. Casting it up, Don Quixote found that it
amounted to sixty-three *reals,* and commanded the
Farmer to pay the money at once, unless he had a mind
to die for it.

This the Farmer, who was in a terrible fright, promised to do, but said he: 'The worst of it is, Sir Knight,
that I have no money here. Let Andrew come with me

to my house, and I will pay him his wages to the last *real.*'

'I go with him?' said the boy, 'evil befall me if I do. No, Sir. I don't intend to do that, for as soon as ever we were alone, he would flay me alive.'

'He will not dare to do it,' said Don Quixote, 'for my command is sufficient to make him respect me. And on condition that he will swear to me to carry out his promise, by the order of Knighthood which he hath received, I will set him free and assure thee of the payment.'

'Good your worship,' said the youth; 'mark well what you say, for this man my master is no Knight, nor did he ever receive any order of Knighthood. He is John Haldudo the rich, and lives at Quintanar.'

'That is no matter,' said Don Quixote, 'for there may be Knights of the Haldudos.'

'The good Knight speaks well, friend Andrew,' said his master. 'Do me but the pleasure to come with me, and I swear by all the orders of Knighthood that are in the world to pay thee, as I have said, to the last *real.*'

'With this,' said Don Quixote, 'I will rest satisfied; and see that thou fulfillest it as thou hast sworn. If not, I swear again to thee by the same oath to return and seek thee out once more and chastise thee. And I will find thee out, though thou didst hide thyself closer than a lizar. And if thou desirest to know who it is that commands thee thus, know that I am the valiant Don Quixote of the Mancha, the righter of wrongs and the scourge of injustice.'

Saying this, the Knight clapt spurs to his Rozinante, and was quickly gone from him.

The Farmer followed him with his eyes, and seeing that he was beyond the wood and quite out of sight, he returned to Andrew and said: 'Come to me, child, for I will pay thee what I owe thee, as that righter of wrongs hath commanded.'

'Upon my word,' said Andrew, 'you do well to fulfil the good Knight's commandments. And I pray that he may live a thousand years, for he is so brave and so just a judge that, if you pay me not, he will come back and do all he promised.'

'I also do believe the same,' said the Farmer; 'but for the much love I bear thee, I will increase the debt that I may add to the payment.'

And seizing him by the arm, he tied him again to the oak, where he gave him so many blows as to leave him for dead.

'Call now, Master Andrew,' said he, 'for thy righter of wrongs; and thou shalt see that he cannot undo this, though I think I have not finished the doing of it, for I have yet a desire to flay thee alive as thou didst fear.'

But he untied him at last, and gave him leave to go and seek out his Judge, to the end that he might execute the sentence he had pronounced. Andrew departed somewhat discontented, swearing to search for the valiant Don Quixote of the Mancha, and relate to him point for point all that had passed, that the Farmer might be repaid sevenfold. Nevertheless he wept as he went

along, and his master remained behind laughing, and
thus did the valiant Don Quixote right this wrong.

As for the Knight, it appeared to him that he had made
a very happy and noble beginning to his feats of arms.
And as he rode toward his village, he recited to himself
in a low voice these words: 'Well mayest thou call thyself happy above all other women of the earth, O! above
all beauties, beautiful Dulcinea of Toboso; since it has
fallen to thy lot to hold submissive to thy will a Knight
so renowned and valorous as is and ever shall be, Don
Quixote of the Mancha, who, as all the world knows,
but yesterday received the order of Knighthood, and to-
day hath destroyed the greatest outrage and wrong that
injustice and cruelty could commit. To-day hath he
wrested the scourge from the hand of the pitiless foe
who so cruelly beat the delicate infant.'

Soon afterwards he came to a spot where the road
branched into four, and there came into his fancy the
cross-ways he had read of where the Knights Errant
used to ponder which of the roads they should take.
And that he might imitate them, he let slip the reins on
Rozinante's neck, submitting his will to that of his steed,
who followed his first intention, which was to return
home to his own stable. And having travelled some two
miles, Don Quixote discovered a great troop of people,
who, as it was afterwards known, were certain merchants
of Toledo, that rode towards Murcia to buy silks. They
were six in number, and came with their parasols or sun
umbrellas, and four serving-men a-horseback, and three
lackeys.

Scarce had Don Quixote perceived them when he straight imagined them to be a new adventure. And so that he might imitate as far as possible the passages which he had read in his books, he settled himself with a gallant air and resolute bearing firmly in his stirrups, grasped his lance, brought his target over his breast, and stood waiting, posted in the middle of the road, for those whom he took to be Knights Errant like himself.

And when they were so near that they might hear and see him, he lifted up his voice and said: 'Let all the world stand and pass no further, if all the world will not confess that there is not in all the world a more beautiful damsel than the Empress of the Mancha, the peerless Dulcinea of Toboso.'

The merchants stopped at the sound of these words to behold the marvellous and ridiculous shape of him that spake them, and at once suspected the madness of the speaker.

Curious to know the meaning of the confession he demanded from them, one of the merchants, who was a bit of a wag and very sharp-witted, said to Don Quixote: 'Sir Knight, we know not who that good lady may be you speak of. Show her therefore to us, and if she be as beautiful as you report, we will with right good-will, and without further trouble, confess the truth of what you demand.'

'If I did show her to you,' replied Don Quixote, 'what merit would there be in confessing a truth which is clear to all beholders? The importance of my demand is that without seeing her you must believe it, which if you

refuse to do I challenge you all to battle, ye proud pre-
posterous crew. And now come on! One by one as the
order of Knighthood requires, or all at once as is the custom and base usage of those of your breed. Here I await
you, confiding in the right I have on my side.'

'Sir Knight,' replied the Merchant, 'I request you in
the name of all the Princes here present, that in order
that we may not burden our conscience by confessing a
thing which we have never beheld nor heard, you will
be pleased to show us some portrait of the lady, although
it be no bigger than a grain of wheat. For I do believe
that we are already so much on your side, that though
her portrait showed her to us a-squint of one eye, and
wearing a hump on her back, we should say all that you
wish in her favour.'

'Infamous rabble,' replied Don Quixote, mightily enraged; 'she is neither crook-eyed nor hump-backed, but
is straighter than a spindle of Guadamara. Dearly shall
you pay for the foul words you have uttered against so
immense a beauty as my Lady.' So saying, he lowered
his lance against him who had spoken, with such wrath
and fury, that if Rozinante had not tripped and fallen
in the midst of his career, it would have fared ill with the
rash Merchant.

But, alas! Rozinante fell; his master went rolling some
distance across the field, and though he struggled to arise
yet was he never able, so encumbered was he by his
lance, spurs, helmet, and the weight of his old-fashioned
armour. And while he strove to rise he shouted; 'Fly not,
cowardly brood! Tarry a little, ye base caitiffs! for not

by any fault of mine, but of my horse, am I thus dis-
comfited!'

One of the lackeys with the company, hearing these
saucy speeches of the poor overthrown Knight, could not
forbear returning him an answer on his ribs, and coming
up to him he seized his lance, and having broken it into
pieces, began with one of them to belabour him, so that
in spite of his armour he pounded him like wheat in a
mill. His masters called out to him to let the gentleman
be, but the lackey was angry and would not give up the
game. And running for the other pieces of the broken
lance, he shivered them all over the poor fallen Knight,
who never closed his mouth, but cried out against them
for brigands and murderers, for such he took them to be.

At last the lackey was tired out, and the merchants
followed on their way talking about the poor belaboured
Knight, who when he saw himself alone, again made
trial to arise; but if he could not do so when sound and
well, how could he after being pounded and almost
beaten to a jelly? And yet he still considered himself
fortunate, for he persuaded himself that this disgrace
was one of those things that must of occasion happen
to a Knight Errant. And though he could not arise on
account of being mauled and bruised from head to foot,
he put it all down the carelessness of his steed Rozinante.

THE·DESTRUCTION
·OF·DON·QUIXOTE'S
·LIBRARY ✤ ✤ ✤

CHAPTER V

How Don Quixote returned home, and what
happened to his Library, and how he sallied
forth a second time to seek Adventures

FINDING that he was unable to stir, the Knight pleased
himself whilst lying on the ground by remembering and
repeating aloud passages from his favourite books.

He was reciting the ballad of the Marquess of Mantua,
in which a noble knight has an adventure similar to his
own, when there chanced to pass by a labouring man, a
neighbour of Don Quixote's, who was going to take a
load of wheat to the mill.

He, seeing a man stretched on the ground, came over

30

to him and asked who he was and what mishap had befallen him.

Don Quixote at once believed that the labourer was no other than the Marquess of Mantua himself, and went on with his ballad which gave an account of his disgrace.

The labourer was astonished at all these foibles, and taking off the Knight's visor, which was all broken to pieces with the beating, he wiped his face, which was covered with dust; and when he had wiped it he recognized him and cried: 'Senor Quixada (for so was he named before he became a Knight Errant), who has brought your Worship to this plight?'

But the Knight only went on with his ballad, and made no answer.

Seeing this, the good man took off as well as he could his breastplate and corselet to see if he had any wound, but he found no blood nor sign of any. He tried to raise him from the ground, which he did at last with much ado. Then he mounted him upon his ass, which seemed a safer carriage than the Knight's steed. Gathering up his arms, even to the fragments of the lance, he fastened them upon Rozinante, whose bridle he took hold of, as well as of the ass's halter; and so they journeyed towards the village, Don Quixote continuing to mutter his nonsensical stories.

In this manner they arrived at last at their village about sunset, but the labourer waited until it grew somewhat dusk, so that folk should not see the Knight so simply mounted.

When he entered the village and went to Don Quixote's house, he found all in uproar there. For the Curate and the Barber—Don Quixote's great friends—were there, and his Housekeeper was crying to them at the top of her voice: 'What think ye has befallen my Master? For two days both he and his horse, together with the target, lance, and armour, have been missing. Woe is me! I am certain those horrid books of Knighthood have turned his brain, for I have often heard him say that he would become a Knight Errant and go and seek adventures throughout the world!'

And Don Quixote's Niece, who was there also, said to Master Nicholas the Barber: 'And indeed I have known my dear Uncle continue reading these unhappy books of "disadventures" two days and two nights together. At the end of which, throwing down the book, he would lay hand on his sword and would fall a-slashing of the walls. And when he was wearied he would say that he had slain four Giants as great as four towers. And I take great blame to myself that I did not tell you all this before, that you might have burned those wretched books which have caused all the mischief.'

'So I say, too,' said the Curate; 'and to-morrow they shall feed the flames, so that they may do no further harm.'

By this time the labourer and Don Quixote had come to the house, and all the household hearing them arrive, ran to embrace him. And Don Quixote—who had not yet dismounted from the ass, for he was not able—said: 'Stand still and touch me not, for I return very sore wounded and hurt through the fault of my steed. Carry me to bed, and summon, if it be possible, the wise Urganda, that she may examine and cure my wounds.'

'Come, my dear Master,' said his Housekeeper, 'and welcome, for, without sending for that Urganda, we shall know how to cure thee well enough. Accursed say I once again, and a hundred times accursed, may those books of Knighthood be which have brought you to such a pass.'

With that they bore him up to his bed, and searching for his wounds could not find any. Then he said he was all one bruise, through having a grievous fall with his horse Rozinante, in a fight with ten Giants, the most enormous and the boldest that could be found on earth.

'So ho!' said the Curate, 'there are Giants about, are there? By mine honesty I will burn them all before to-morrow night.'

The next day, while the Knight was asleep, the Curate asked the Niece for the keys of the library, which she gave him with a very good will. Then they all went in, the Housekeeper with them, and found more than a hundred very large volumes well bound, besides other smaller ones.

The Curate asked the Barber to hand him down the books from their shelves one by one, that he might see whether any deserved to escape the fire.

'No, no!' cried the Niece, 'you ought not to pardon any of them, seeing they have all been offenders. Better fling them all out of the window into the yard and make a heap of them, and then make a bonfire of them where the smoke will offend nobody.'

With that the Housekeeper caught hold of some of the largest and flung them out of the window. But the Curate took down several from the shelves and began to examine them carefully, whilst the women cried out for their destruction.

Whilst they were thus busied, Don Quixote began to cry aloud, saying: 'This way, this way, valorous Knights! Show the force of your valiant arms lest we lose the tournament.'

Called away by this noise and clamour they left the books and ran to Don Quixote, who had risen from his bed and was repeating his outcries and ravings, cutting about with his sword all over the room with slashes and back strokes, as wide awake as if he had never been asleep. Wherefore, taking him up in their arms, they returned him by main force into his bed.

With some difficulty they persuaded him to rest where he was, and after he had eaten his breakfast he fell asleep once again.

That same night the Housekeeper set fire to and burned all the books in the yard, and some went to the flames that had no harm in them; and thus was fulfilled the old proverb, 'The Saint sometimes pays for the Sinner.'

Now one of the remedies which the Curate and the Barber suggested for their friend's malady was to wall up and close his library, so that when he rose he should not find the books, and they might tell him the Enchanters had carried them off, room and all.

This was done, and when two days afterwards Don

Quixote rose from his bed, the first thing he did was to go and visit his books. Not finding the library where he had left it, he went from one corner of the house to the other looking for it. Sometimes he came to the place where the door had been, and felt it with his hands, then would turn his eyes up and down, here and there, to seek it, without speaking a word.

But at last he asked the Housekeeper where his library was. She being well schooled what she should answer, replied: 'What library? There is neither library nor books in this house now, for an Enchanter has carried them all away.'

'Yes, dear Uncle,' said his Niece, 'while you were away, an Enchanter came upon a cloud, and, alighting from a serpent on which he was riding, entered the library, and what he did therein I know not. But within a while after, he fled out at the roof of the house, and left all the place full of smoke, and when we went to see what he had done we found neither room nor books.'

'This must be the work of the learned Enchanter Freston,' replied Don Quixote seriously; 'a great enemy of mine who has a grudge against me, for he knows through his arts and his learning that I am in course of time to fight and vanquish in single combat a Knight whom he favours. But I tell him it is useless to oppose what is decreed.'

'Who doubts that, dear Uncle?' said his Niece. 'But why mix yourself up in these quarrels? Better stay at home peacefully, for remember the proverb says, "Many who go for wool come back shorn."'

'O Niece of mine,' said Don Quixote, 'how little dost thou understand the matter! Before I am shorn I will pluck the beards of all who think to touch but a hair of me.'

To these words the women made no reply because they saw his anger increase.

For fifteen days after this he remained quietly at home, without showing any signs of repeating his follies, and during this time he had many arguments with his friends the Curate and the Barber about his favourite Knights Errant. At the same time he was persuading a certain labourer, his neighbour, an honest man, but one of very shallow wit, to go away with him and serve him as Squire. In the end he gave him so many fair words and promises that the poor fellow determined to go with him. Don Quixote, among other things, told him that he ought to be very pleased to depart with him, for at some time or other an adventure might befall which should in the twinkling of an eye win him an Island and leave him Governor thereof. On the faith of these and other like promises, Sancho Panza (for so he was called) forsook his wife and children and took service as Squire to his neighbour.

Don Quixote then set about to provide himself with money. This he did by selling one thing, pawning another, and making bad bargains all round. At last he got a pretty sum, and having patched up his broken helmet as best he could, he told Sancho Panza the day and hour on which he meant to start. He also charged him to provide himself with a wallet, which Sancho promised to do, and said that he also meant to take a very good Ass named Dapple along with him, which he had of his own, because he was not used to travel much afoot.

In the matter of the Ass, Don Quixote hesitated a little, calling to mind whether ever he had read that any Knight Errant was ever attended by a Squire mounted on ass-back, but no such case occurred to his memory. Nevertheless, he decided that the Ass should be taken, with the intention of providing his Squire with a more dignified mount, when he had a chance, by unhorsing the first discourteous Knight he met with.

All this being arranged, Sancho Panza, without bidding his wife and children farewell, and Don Quixote, without saying good-bye to his Housekeeper and Niece, sallied forth from the village one night, unknown to any person living. They travelled so far that night that at daybreak they were safe against discovery, even if they were pursued. And Sancho Panza rode along on his beast like a patriarch with his wallet and bottle, full of a huge desire to see himself Governor of the Island which his Master had promised him.

CHAPTER VI

Of the dreadful and never-to-be-imagined Adventure of the Windmills, and of the fearful Battle which the gallant Biscayan fought with Don Quixote

WHILST they were journeying along, Sancho Panza said to his Master: 'I pray you have good care, Sir Knight, that you forget not that government of the Island which you have promised me, for I shall be able to govern it be it never so great.'

And Don Quixote replied: 'Thou must understand, friend Sancho, that it was a custom very much used by ancient Knights Errant, to make their Squires Governors of the Islands and Kingdoms they conquered, and I am resolved that so good a custom shall be kept up by me. And if thou livest and I live it may well be that I might conquer a Kingdom within six days, and crown thee King of it.'

'By the same token,' said Sancho Panza, 'if I were a King, then should Joan my wife become a Queen and my children Princes?'

'Who doubts of that?' said Don Quixote.

'That do I,' replied Sancho Panza, 'for I am fully per-

DON QUIXOTE
AND THE WINDMILLS

suaded that though it rained Kingdoms down upon the earth, none of them would sit well on my wife Joan. She is not worth a farthing for a Queen. She might scrape through as a Countess, but I have my doubts of that.'

As they were talking, they caught sight of some thirty or forty windmills on a plain. As soon as Don Quixote saw them he said to his Squire: 'Fortune is guiding our affairs better than we could desire. For behold, friend Sancho, how there appear thirty or forty monstrous Giants with whom I mean to do battle, and take all their lives. With their spoils we will begin to be rich, for this is fair war, and it is doing great service to clear away these evil fellows from off the face of the earth.'

'What Giants?' said Sancho amazed.

'Those thou seest there,' replied his Master, 'with the long arms.'

'Take care, Sir,' cried Sancho, 'for those we see yonder are not Giants but windmills, and those things which seem to be arms are their sails, which being whirled round by the wind make the mill go.'

'It is clear,' answered Don Quixote, 'that thou art not yet experienced in the matter of adventures. They are Giants, and if thou art afraid, get thee away home, whilst I enter into cruel and unequal battle with them.'

So saying, he clapped spurs to Rozinante, without heeding the cries by which Sancho Panza warned him that he was going to encounter not Giants but windmills. For he would neither listen to Sancho's outcries, nor mark what he said, but shouted to the windmills in a loud voice: 'Fly not, cowards and vile creatures, for it is only one Knight that assaults you!'

A slight breeze having sprung up at this moment, the great sail-arms began to move, on seeing which Don Quixote shouted out again: 'Although you should wield more arms than had the Giant Briareus, I shall make you pay for your insolence!'

Saying this, and commending himself most devoutly to his Lady Dulcinea, whom he desired to aid him in this peril, covering himself with his buckler, and setting his lance in rest, he charged at Rozinante's best gallop, and attacked the first mill before him. Thrusting his lance through the sail, the wind turned it with such violence that it broke his weapon into shivers, carrying him and his horse after it, and having whirled them round, finally tumbled the Knight a good way off, and rolled him over the plain sorely damaged.

Sancho Panza hastened to help him as fast as his Ass could go, and when he came up he found the Knight unable to stir, such a shock had Rozinante given him in the fall.

'Bless me,' said Sancho, 'did I not tell you that you should look well what you did, for they were none other than windmills, nor could any think otherwise unless he had windmills in his brains?'

'Peace, friend Sancho,' said Don Quixote, 'for the things of war are constantly changing, and I think this must be the work of the same sage Freston who robbed me of my library and books, and he hath changed these Giants into windmills to take from me the glory of the victory. But in the end his evil arts shall avail but little against the goodness of my sword.'

'May it prove so,' said Sancho, as he helped his Master to rise and remount Rozinante, who, poor steed, was himself much bruised by the fall.

The next day they journeyed along towards the Pass of Lapice, a romantic spot, at which they arrived about three o'clock in the afternoon.

'Here,' said Don Quixote to his Squire, 'we may hope to dip our hands up to the elbows in what are called adventures. But take note of this, that although thou seest me in the greatest dangers of the world, thou art not to set hand to thy sword in my defence, unless those who assault me be base or vulgar people. If they be Knights thou mayest not help me.'

'I do assure you, Sir,' said Sancho, 'that herein you shall be most punctually obeyed, because I am by nature a quiet and peaceful man, and have a strong dislike to thrusting myself into quarrels.'

Whilst they spoke thus, two Friars of the order of St. Benedict, mounted on large mules—big enough to be dromedaries—appeared coming along the road. They wore travelling masks to keep the dust out of their eyes and carried large sun-umbrellas. After them came a coach with four or five a-horseback travelling with it, and two lackeys ran hard by it. In the coach was a Biscayan Lady who was going to Seville. The Friars were not of her company, though all were going the same way.

Scarcely had Don Quixote espied them than he exclaimed to his Squire: 'Either I much mistake, or this

should be the most famous adventure that hath ever
been seen; for those dark forms that loom yonder are
doubtless Enchanters who are carrying off in that coach
some Princess they have stolen. Therefore I must with
all my power undo this wrong.'

'This will be worse than the adventure of the windmills,' said Sancho. 'Do you not see that they are Bene-
dictine Friars, and the coach will belong to some people
travelling?'

'I have told thee already, Sancho,' answered Don
Quixote, 'that thou are very ignorant in the matter of
adventures. What I say is true, as thou shalt see.'

So saying he spurred on his horse, and posted himself
in the middle of the road along which the Friars were
coming, and when they were near enough to hear him
he exclaimed in a loud voice: 'Monstrous and horrible
crew! Surrender this instant those exalted Princesses,
whom you are carrying away in that coach, or prepare
to receive instant death as a just punishment of your
wicked deeds.'

The Friars drew rein, and stood amazed at the figure
and words of Don Quixote to whom they replied: 'Sir
Knight, we are neither monstrous nor wicked, but two
religious men, Benedictines, travelling about our business, and we know nothing about this coach or about
any Princesses.'

'No soft words for me,' cried Don Quixote, 'for I know
you well, treacherous knaves.'

And without waiting for their reply he set spurs to
Rozinante; and laying his lance on his thigh, charged at

the first Friar with such fury and rage, that if he had not leaped from his mule he would have been slain, or at least badly wounded.

The second Friar, seeing the way his companion was treated, made no words but fled across the country swifter than the wind itself.

Sancho Panza, on seeing the Friar overthrown, dismounted very speedily off his Ass and ran over to him, and would have stripped him of his clothes. But two of the Friar's servants came up and asked him why he was thus despoiling their master. Sancho replied that it was due by the law of arms, as lawful spoils gained in battle by his Lord and Master, Don Quixote.

The lackeys, who knew nothing of battles or spoils, seeing that Don Quixote was now out of the way, speaking with those that were in the coach, set both at once upon Sancho and threw him down, plucked every hair out of his beard and kicked and mauled him without mercy, leaving him at last stretched on the ground senseless and breathless.

As for the Friar, he mounted again, trembling and terror-stricken, all the colour having fled from his face, and spurring his mule, he joined his companion, who was waiting for him hard by.

While this was happening, Don Quixote was talking to the Lady in the coach, to whom he said: 'Dear Lady, you may now dispose of yourself as you best please. For the pride of your robbers is laid in the dust by this my invincible arm. And that you may not pine to learn the name of your deliverer, know that I am called Don Quixote of the Mancha, Knight Errant, adventurer, and captive of the peerless and beauteous Lady Dulcinea of Toboso. And in reward of the benefits you have received at my hands, I demand nothing else but that you return to Toboso, there to present yourself in my name before my Lady, and tell her what I have done to obtain your liberty.'

All this was listened to by a Biscayan Squire who accompanied the coach. He hearing that the coach was not to pass on but was to return to Toboso, went up to Don Quixote, and, laying hold of his lance, said to him: 'Get away with thee, Sir Knight, for if thou leave not the coach I will kill thee as sure as I am a Biscayan.'

'If,' replied Don Quixote haughtily, 'thou wert a gentleman, as thou art not, I would ere this have punished thy folly and insolence, caitiff creature.'

'I no gentleman?' cried the enraged Biscayan. 'Throw down thy lance and draw thy sword, and thou shalt soon see that thou liest.'

'That shall be seen presently,' replied Don Quixote; and flinging his lance to the ground he drew his sword, grasped his buckler tight, and rushed at the Biscayan.

The Biscayan, seeing him come on in this manner, had nothing else to do but to draw his sword. Luckily for him he was near the coach, whence he snatched a cushion to serve him as a shield, and then they fell on one another as if they had been mortal enemies.

Those that were present tried to stop them, but the Biscayan shouted out that if he were hindered from ending the battle he would put his Lady and all who touched him to the sword.

The Lady, amazed and terrified, made the coachman draw aside a little, and sat watching the deadly combat from afar.

The Biscayan, to begin with, dealt Don Quixote a mighty blow over the target, which, if it had not been for his armour, would have cleft him to the waist. Don Quixote, feeling the weight of this tremendous blow which had destroyed his visor and carried away part of his ear, cried out aloud: 'O Dulcinea, Lady of my soul, flower of all beauty, help thy Knight, who finds himself in this great danger!' To say this, to raise his sword, to cover himself with his buckler, and to rush upon the Biscayan was the work of a moment. With his head full of rage he now raised himself in his stirrups, and, gripping his sword more firmly in his two hands struck at the Biscayan with such violence that he caught him a terrible blow on the cushion, knocking this shield against his head with tremendous violence. It was as though a mountain had fallen on the Biscayan and crushed him, and the blood spouted from his nose and mouth and ears. He would have fallen straightway from his mule if he had not clasped her round the neck; but he lost his stirrups, then let go his arms, and the mule, frightened at the blow, began to gallop across the fields, so that after two or three plunges it threw him to the ground.

Don Quixote leaped off his horse, ran towards him, and setting the point of his sword between his eyes, bade him yield, or he would cut off his head.

The Lady of the coach now came forward in great grief and begged the favour of her Squire's life.

Don Quixote replied with great stateliness: 'Truly fair Lady, I will grant thy request, but it must be on one condition, that this Squire shall go to Toboso and present himself in my name to the peerless Lady Dulcinea, that she may deal with him as she thinks well.'

The Lady, who was in great distress, without considering what Don Quixote required, or asking who Dulcinea might be, promised that he should certainly perform this command.

'Then,' said Don Quixote, 'on the faith of that pledge I will do him no more harm.'

Seeing the contest was now over, and his Master about to remount Rozinante, Sancho ran to hold his stirrups, and before he mounted, taking him by his hand he kissed it and said: 'I desire that it will please you, good my Lord Don Quixote, to bestow on me the government of that Island which in this terrible battle you have won.'

To which Don Quixote replied: 'Brother Sancho, these are not the adventures of Islands, but of cross roads, wherein nothing is gained by a broken pate or the loss of an ear. Have patience awhile, for the adventures will come whereby I can make thee not only a Governor, but something higher.'

Sancho thanked him heartily, and kissed his hand again and the hem of his mailed shirt. Then he helped him to get on Rozinante, and leaped upon his Ass to follow him.

And Don Quixote, without another word to the people of the coach, rode away at a swift pace and turned into a wood that was hard by, leaving Sancho to follow him as fast as his beast could trot.

CHAPTER VII

Of what passed between Don Quixote and the
Goatherds, and of the unfortunate Adventure
with the Yanguesian Carriers

As they rode along, Don Quixote turned to his Squire
and said to him: 'Tell me now in very good earnest, didst
thou ever see a more valorous Knight than I am throughout the face of the earth? Didst thou ever read in histories of any other that hath or ever had more courage
in fighting, more dexterity in wounding, or more skill in
overthrowing?'

'The truth is,' replied Sancho, 'that I have never read
any history whatever, for I can neither read nor write.
But what I dare wager is, that I never in my life served
a bolder Master than you are, and I only trust that all
this boldness does not land us within the four walls of
the gaol.'

'Peace, friend Sancho,' said Don Quixote; 'when didst
thou read of a Knight Errant that was brought before
the Judge though he killed ever so many people?'

'I have read nothing, as you know, good Master; but
a truce to all this, let me attend to your wound, for you
are losing a good deal of blood in that ear, and I have

DON QUIXOTE
AND THE GOATHERDS

got some lint and a little white ointment in my wallet.'

'That,' said Don Quixote, 'would have been unnecessary if I had remembered to make a bottleful of the Balsam of Fierabras, for with only one drop of it both time and medicines are saved.'

'What Balsam is that, then?' asked Sancho Panza.

'It is a Balsam, the receipt of which I have in my memory, and whoever possesses it need not fear death nor think to perish by any wound. Therefore after I have made it and given it unto thee, thou hast nothing else to do but when thou shalt see that in any battle I be cloven in twain, than deftly to take up the portion of the body which is fallen to the ground and put it up again on the half which remains in the saddle, taking great care to fix it exactly in the right place. Then thou shalt give me two draughts of the Balsam I have mentioned, and I shall become as sound as an apple.'

'If that be true,' said Sancho, 'I renounce from now the government of the promised Island, and will demand nothing else in payment of my services but only the receipt of this precious liquor. But tell me, is it costly in making?'

'With less than three *reals*,' said Don Quixote, 'a man may make three gallons of it. But I mean to teach thee greater secrets than this, and do thee greater favours also. And now let me dress my wound, for this ear pains me more than I would wish.'

Sancho took out of his wallet his lint and ointment to cure his Master. But before he could use them Don Quixote saw that the visor of his helmet was broken, and he had like to have lost his senses. Setting his hand to his sword, he cried: 'I swear on oath to lead the life which was led by the great Marquis of Mantua when he swore to revenge the death of his nephew Baldwin, which was not to eat off a tablecloth, nor to comb his hair, nor to change his clothes, nor to quit his armour, and other things which, though I cannot now remember, I take as said, until I have had complete revenge on him that hath done this outrage.'

'Look, your Worship, Sir Don Quixote,' said Sancho, when he heard these strange words, 'you must note that if the Biscayan has done what you told him, and presented himself before my Lady Dulcinea of Toboso, then he has fully satisfied his debt, and deserves no other penalty unless he commits a new fault.'

'Thou hast spoken well and hit the mark truly,' answered Don Quixote; 'and, therefore, in respect of that, I set the oath aside. But I make it and confirm it again, that I will lead the life I have said, until I take by force another helmet as good as this from some other Knight.'

'Such oaths are but mischief,' said Sancho discontentedly, 'for tell me now, if by chance we do not come across a man armed with a helmet, what are we to do? Do but consider that armed men travel not these roads, but only carriers and waggoners, who not only wear no helmets, but never heard them named all the days of their life.'

'Thou art mistaken in this,' said Don Quixote, 'for we shall not have been here two hours before we shall see more Knights than went up against Albraca to win Angelica the Fair.'

'So be it,' said Sancho, 'and may all turn out well for us, that the time may come for the winning of that Island which is costing me so dear.'

'Have no fear for thine Island, Sancho Panza,' said Don Quixote; 'and now look if thou hast aught to eat in thy wallet, for soon we should go in search of some Castle where we may lodge the night and make the Balsam of which I have spoken, for in truth this ear of mine pains me greatly.'

'I have got here an onion and a bit of cheese and a few crusts of bread, but such coarse food is not fit for so valiant a Knight as your Worship.'

'How little dost thou understand the matter,' replied Don Quixote, 'for it is an honour to Knights Errant not to eat more than once a month, and if by chance they should eat, to eat only of that which is next at hand! And all this thou mightest have known hadst thou read as many books as I have done. For though I studied many, yet did I never find that Knights Errant did ever eat but by mere chance, or at some costly banquets that were made for them. And the remainder of their days they lived on herbs and roots. Therefore, friend Sancho, let not that trouble thee which is my pleasure, for to a Knight Errant that which comes is good.'

'Pardon me, Sir,' said Sancho, 'for since I can neither read nor write, as I have already told you, I have not fallen in rightly with the laws of Knighthood. But from henceforth my wallet shall be furnished with all sorts of dried fruits for your Worship, because you are a Knight, and for myself, seeing I am none, I will provide fowls and other things, which are better eating.'

So saying he pulled out what he had, and the two fell to dinner in good peace and company.

But being desirous to look out for a lodging for that night, they cut short their meagre and sorry meal, mounted at once a-horseback, and made haste to find out some dwellings before night did fall.

But the sun and their hopes did fail them at the same time, they being then near the cabins of some Goatherds. Therefore they determined to pass the night there. And though Sancho's grief was great to lie out of a village, yet Don Quixote was more joyful than ever, for he thought that as often as he slept under the open heaven, so often did he perform an act worthy of a true Knight Errant.

They were welcomed by the Goatherds very cordially, and Sancho, having put up Rozinante and his Ass the best way he could, made his way towards the smell given out by certain pieces of goat's flesh which were boiling in a pot on the fire. And though he longed that very instant to see if they were ready, he did not do so, for he saw the Goatherds were themselves taking them off the fire and spreading some sheep-skins on the ground, and were laying their rustic table as quickly as might be. Then with many expressions of good will they invited the two to share in what they had. Those who belonged to the fold, being six in number, sat round on the skins, having first with rough compliments asked Don Quixote to seat himself upon a trough which they placed for him turned upside down.

Don Quixote sat down, but Sancho remained on foot to serve him with the cup which was made of horn. Seeing him standing, his Master said: 'That thou mayest see, Sancho, the good which is in Knight Errantry, and how fair a chance they have who exercise it to arrive at honour and position in the world, I desire that here by my side, and in company of these good people, thou dost seat thyself, and be one and the same with me that am thy Master and natural Lord. That thou dost eat in my dish and drink in the same cup wherein I drink. For the same may be said of Knight Errantry as is said of Love, that it makes all things equal.'

'Thanks for your favour,' replied Sancho, 'but I may tell your Worship that provided I have plenty to eat, I can eat it as well, and better, standing and by myself, than if I were seated on a level with an Emperor. And, indeed, if I speak the truth, what I eat in my corner without ceremony, though it be but a bread and onion, smacks much better than turkey-cocks at other tables, where I must chaw my meat leisurely, drink but little, wipe my hands often, nor do other things that solitude and liberty allow.'

'For all that,' said Don Quixote, 'here shalt thou sit, for the humble shall be exalted,' and taking him by the arm, he forced his Squire to sit down near himself.

The Goatherds did not understand the gibberish of Squires and Knights Errant, and did nothing but eat, hold their peace, and stare at their guests, who with great relish were gorging themselves with pieces as big as their fists. The course of flesh being over, the Goatherds spread on the skins a great number of parched acorns and half a cheese, harder than if it had been made of mortar. The horn in the meantime was not idle, but came full from the wine-skins and returned empty, as though it had been a bucket sent to the well.

After Don Quixote had satisfied his appetite, he took up a fistful of acorns, and beholding them earnestly, began in this manner: 'Happy time and fortunate ages were those which our ancestors called Golden, not because Gold—so much prized in this our Iron Age—was gotten in that happy time without any labours, but because those who lived in that time knew not these two words, *Thine* and *Mine*. In that holy age all things were in common. No man needed to do aught but lift up his hand and take his food from the strong oak, which did liberally invite them to gather his sweet and savoury fruit. The clear fountains and running rivers did offer then transparent water in magnificent abundance, and in the hollow trees did careful bees erect their commonwealth, offering to every hand without interest the fertile crop of their sweet labours.' Thus did the eloquent Knight describe the Golden Age, when all was peace, friendship, and concord, and then he showed the astonished Goatherds how an evil world had taken its place, and made it necessary for Knights Errant like himself to come forward for the protection of widows and orphans, and the defence of distressed damsels. All this he did because the acorns that were given him called to his mind the Golden Age. The Goatherds sat and listened with grave attention, and Sancho made frequent visits to the second wine-skin during his discourse. At length it was ended, and they sat round the fire, drinking their wine and listening to one of the Goatherds singing, and towards night, Don Quixote's ear becoming very painful, one of his hosts made a dressing of rosemary leaves and salt, and bound up his wound. By this means being eased of his pain, he was able to lie down in one of the huts and sleep soundly after his day's adventures.

Don Quixote spent several days among the Goatherds, and at length, when his wound was better, he thanked them for their hospitality, and rode away in search of new adventures, followed by the faithful Sancho.

They came to a halt in a pleasant meadow rich with beautiful grass, by the side of a delightful and refreshing stream, which seemed to invite them to stop and spend there the sultry hours of noon, which were already becoming oppressive.

Don Quixote and Sancho dismounted, and leaving Rozinante and Dapple loose, to feed on the grass that was there in plenty, they ransacked the wallet, and without any ceremony fell to eating what they found in it.

Sancho had neglected to tie up Rozinante, and, as luck would have it, a troop of Galician ponies belonging to some Yanguesian carriers, whose custom it is to rest at noon with their teams in spots and places where grass and water abound, were feeding in the same valley.

It must be believed that Rozinante supposed that the grass the ponies were feeding on was better than his own; but be that as it may, he started off at a little swift trot to feed among them. They resented his appearance, and, as he sought to enter their ranks and feed among them, they received him with their heels and teeth, with such vigour that in a trice he had burst his girth, and his saddle was stripped from his back. But the worst of all was that the carriers, taking part with their own ponies, ran up with stakes and so belaboured him that they brought him to the ground in a sore plight.

Upon this Don Quixote and Sancho, who witnessed the basting of Rozinante, came running up all out of breath, and Don Quixote said to Sancho: 'From what I see, friend Sancho, these be no Knights, but base, rascally fellows of low breeding. I say this, that thou mayest freely aid me in taking vengeance for the wrong which they have done to Rozinante before our eyes.'

'What vengeance can we take,' replied Sancho, 'when there are more than twenty, and we are but two—nay, perhaps but one and a half?'

'I count for a hundred,' said Don Quixote, and without further parley he drew his sword and flew upon the Yanguesians, boldly followed by Sancho Panza. With his first blow Don Quixote pierced a buff coat that one of them wore, wounding him grievously in the shoulder. Then the Yanguesians, finding themselves so rudely handled by two men only, they being so many, betook themselves to their stakes, and hemming in their adversaries in the midst of them, they laid on with great fury. In fact the second thwack brought Sancho to the ground, and the same fate soon befell Don Quixote, whose dexterity and courage availed him nothing, for he fell at the feet of his unfortunate steed, who had not yet been able to arise.

Then seeing the mischief they had done, the Yanguesians loaded their team with as much haste as possible, and went their way, leaving the adventurers in a doleful plight and worse humour.

THE MANNER
OF DON QUIXOTE'S
TRAVEL TO THE INN

CHAPTER VIII

How Don Quixote arrived at an Inn which he
imagined to be a Castle, and there cured himself and Sancho with the Balsam of Fierabras

FOR some time after the Yanguesian Carriers had gone
on their way Don Quixote and Sancho Panza lay on the
ground groaning and saying nothing.

The first that came to himself was Sancho Panza, who
cried in a weak and pitiful voice: 'Sir Don Quixote! O Sir
Don Quixote!'

'What wouldst thou, brother Sancho?' answered Don
Quixote in the same faint and grievous tone as Sancho.

'I would, if it were possible,' said Sancho Panza, 'that

your Worship should give me a couple of mouthfuls of that Balsam of Fierabras, if so be that your Worship has it at hand. Perhaps it will be as good for broken bones as for wounds.'

'If I had it here,' sighed Don Quixote, 'we should lack nothing. But I swear to thee, Sancho Panza, on the faith of a Knight Errant, that before two days pass, unless fortune forbids, I will have it in my possession.'

'I pray you,' asked Sancho, 'in how many days do you think we shall be able to move our feet?'

'I cannot say,' said the battered Knight; 'but I take on myself the blame of all, for I should not have drawn my sword against men that are not Knights. Therefore, brother Sancho, take heed of what I tell thee, for it mightily concerns the welfare of us both; and it is this, that when thou seest such rabble offer us any wrong, wait not for me to draw sword upon them, for I will not do it in any wise, but put thou thy hand to thy sword and chastise them at thy pleasure.'

But Sancho Panza did not much relish his Master's advice, and replied: 'Sir, I am a peaceable, sober, and quiet man, and can let pass any injury whatever, for I have a wife and children to take care of. Therefore, let me also say a word to your Worship, that by no manner of means shall I put hand to sword either against Clown or against Knight. And from this time forth I forgive whatever insults are paid to me, whether they are or shall be paid by persons high or low, rich or poor, gentle or simple.'

On hearing this his Master said: 'Would that I had breath enough to be able to speak easily, and that the pain I feel in this rib were less, that I might make thee understand, Sancho, the mistake thou art making! How can I appoint thee Governor of an Island when thou wouldst make an end of all by having neither valour nor will to defend thy lands or revenge thine injuries?'

'Alas!' groaned Sancho, 'I would that I had the courage and understanding of which your Worship speaks, but in truth at this moment I am more fit for plasters than preachments. See if your Worship can rise, and we will help Rozinante, although he deserves it not, for he was the chief cause of all this mauling.'

'Fortune always leaves one door open in disasters, and your Dapple will now be able to supply the want of Rozinante and carry me hence to some Castle where I may be healed of my wounds. Nor shall I esteem such riding a dishonour, for I remember to have read that old Silenus, tutor and guide of the merry God of Laughter, when he entered the City of a hundred gates, rode very pleasantly, mounted on a handsome ass.'

'That may be,' replied Sancho, 'but there is a difference between riding a-horseback and being laid athwart like a sack of rubbish.'

'Have done with your replies,' exclaimed Don Quixote, 'and rise as well as thou art able and sit me on top of thine Ass, and let us depart hence before the night comes and overtakes us in this wilderness.'

Then Sancho, with thirty groans and sixty sighs and a hundred and twenty curses, lifted up Rozinante—who if he had had a tongue would have complained louder than Sancho himself—and after much trouble set Don

Quixote on the Ass. Then tying Rozinante to his tail, he led the Ass by the halter, and proceeded as best he could to where the highroad seemed to lie.

And Fortune, which had guided their affairs from good to better, led him on to a road on which he spied an Inn, which to his annoyance and Don Quixote's joy must needs be a Castle. Sancho protested that it was an Inn, and his Master that it was a Castle; and their dispute lasted so long that they had time to arrive there before it was finished; and into this Inn or Castle Sancho entered without more parley with all his team.

The Innkeeper, seeing Don Quixote laid athwart of the Ass, asked Sancho what ailed him. Sancho answered that it was nothing, only that he had fallen down from a rock, and had bruised his ribs somewhat. The Innkeeper's wife was by nature charitable, and she felt for the sufferings of others, so she hastened at once to attend to Don Quixote, and made her daughter, a comely young maiden, help her in taking care of her guest. There was also serving in the Inn an Asturian wench, broad-cheeked, flat-pated, with a snub nose, blind of one eye and the other not very sound. This young woman, who was called Maritornes, assisted the daughter, and the two made up a bed for Don Quixote in a garret which had served for many years as a straw-loft. The bed on which they placed him was made of four roughly planed boards on two unequal trestles; a mattress which, in thinness, might have been a quilt, so full of pellets that if they had not through the holes shown themselves to be wool, they would to the touch seem to be pebbles. There was a pair of sheets made of target leather; and as for the coverlet, if any one had chosen to count the threads of it he could not have missed one in the reckoning.

On this miserable bed did Don Quixote lie, and presently the Hostess and her daughter plastered him over from head to foot, Maritornes holding the candle for them.

While she was plastering him, the Hostess, seeing that he was in places black and blue, said that it looked more like blows than a fall. Sancho, however, declared they were not blows, but that the rock had many sharp points, and each one had left a mark; and he added: 'Pray, good Mistress, spare some of that tow, as my back pains are not a little.'

'In that case,' said the Hostess, 'you must have fallen too.'

'I did not fall,' said Sancho Panza, 'but with the sudden fright I took on seeing my Master fall, my body aches as if they had given me a thousand blows, and I now find myself with only a few bruises less than my Master, Don Quixote.'

'What is this gentleman's name?' asked Maritornes.

'Don Quixote of the Mancha,' answered Sancho Panza; 'and he is a Knight Errant, and one of the best and strongest that have been seen in the world these many ages.'

'What is a Knight Errant?' asked the wench.

'Art thou so young in the world that thou knowest it not?' answered Sancho Panza. 'Know then, Sister mine, that a Knight Errant is a thing which in two words is found cudgelled and an Emperor. To-day he is the most miserable creature in the world, and the most needy; to-morrow he will have two or three crowns of Kingdoms to give to his Squire.'

'How is it, then,' said the Hostess, 'that thou hast not gotten at least an Earldom, seeing thou art Squire to this good Knight?'

'It is early yet,' replied Sancho, 'for it is but a month since we set out on our adventures. But believe me, if my Master, Don Quixote, gets well of his wounds—or his fall, I should say—I would not sell my hopes for the best title in Spain.'

To all this Don Quixote listened very attentively, and sitting up in his bed as well as he could, he took the Hostess's hand and said: 'Believe me, beautiful Lady, that you may count yourself fortunate in having entertained me in this your Castle. My Squire will inform you who I am, for self-praise is no recommendation; only this I say, that I will keep eternally written in memory the service you have done to me, and I will be grateful to you as long as my life shall endure.'

The Hostess, her daughter, and the good Maritornes remained confounded on hearing the words of the Knight Errant, which they understood as well as if he had spoken in Greek, but yet they believed they were words of compliment, and so they thanked him for his courtesy and departed, leaving Sancho and his Master for the night.

There happened to be lodging in the Inn that night one of the Officers of the Holy Brotherhood of Toledo, whose duty it was to travel the roads and inquire into cases of highway robbery. He hearing some time later that a man was lying in the house sorely wounded must needs go and make an examination of the matter. He therefore lighted his lamp and made his way to Don Quixote's garret.

As soon as Sancho Panza saw him enter arrayed in a shirt and a nightcap with the lamp in his hand, which showed him to be a very ugly man, he asked his Master: 'Will this by chance be some Wizard Moor come to torment us?'

'A Wizard it cannot be,' said Don Quixote, 'for those under enchantment never let themselves be seen.'

The Officer could make nothing of their talk, and came up to Don Quixote, who lay face upwards encased in his plasters. 'Well,' said the Officer roughly, 'how goes it, my good fellow?'

'I would speak more politely if I were you,' answered Don Quixote. 'Is it the custom in this country, lout, to speak in that way to a Knight Errant?'

The Officer, finding himself thus rudely addressed, could not endure it, and, lifting up the lamp, oil and all, gave Don Quixote such a blow on the pate with it that he broke his head in one or two places, and, leaving all in darkness, left the room.

'Ah!' groaned Sancho, 'this is indeed the Wizard Moor, and he must be keeping his treasures for others, and for us nothing but blows.'

'It is ever so,' replied Don Quixote; 'and we must take

no notice of these things of enchantment, nor must we be angry or vexed with them, for since they are invisible, Sancho, if thou canst, and call the Constable of this fortress, and try to get him to give me a little wine, oil, salt, and rosemary to prepare the health-giving Balsam, of which I have grievous need, for there comes much blood from the wound which the phantom hath given me.'

Sancho arose, not without aching bones, and crept in the dark to where the Innkeeper was, and said to him: 'My Lord Constable, do us the favour and courtesy to give me a little rosemary, oil, wine, and salt to cure one of the best Knights Errant in the world, who lies yonder in bed sorely wounded at the hands of a Moorish Enchanter.'

When the Innkeeper heard this he took Sancho Panza for a man out of his wits, but nevertheless gave him what he wanted, and Sancho carried it to Don Quixote. His Master was lying with his hands to his head, groaning with pain from the blows of the lamp, which, however, had only raised two big lumps; what he thought was blood being only the perspiration running down his face.

He now took the things Sancho had brought, of which he made a compound, mixing them together and boiling them a good while until they came to perfection.

Then he asked for a phial into which to pour this precious liquor, but as there was not one to be had in the Inn, he decided to pour it into a tin oil-vessel which the Innkeeper had given him.

This being done, he at once made an experiment on

himself of the virtue of this precious Balsam, as he imagined it to be, and drank off a whole quart of what was left in the boiling-pot.

The only result of this was that it made him very sick indeed, as well it might, and, what with the sickness and the bruising and the weariness of body, he fell fast asleep for several hours, and at the end of his sleep awoke so refreshed and so much the better of his bruises that he took himself to be cured, and verily believed he had hit upon the Balsam of Fierabras.

Sancho Panza, to whom his Master's recovery seemed little short of a miracle, begged that he might have what was left in the boiling-pot, which was no small quantity. Don Quixote consenting, he took the pot in both hands, and tossed it down, swallowing very little less than his Master had done.

It happened, however, that Sancho's stomach was not so delicate as his Master's and he had suffered such terrible pains and misery before he was sick that he thought his last hour was come, and cursed the Balsam and the thief who had given it to him.

Don Quixote, seeing him in this bad way, said: 'I believe, Sancho, that all this evil befalleth thee because thou are not dubbed Knight, for I am persuaded that this Balsam may not benefit any one that is not.'

'If your Worship knew that,' replied poor Sancho, 'bad luck to me and mine, why did you let me taste it?'

Before Don Quixote could reply to this, Sancho became so terribly sick that he could only lie groaning and moaning for two hours, at the end of which he felt so shaken and shattered that he could scarcely stand, and sadly wished that he had never become Squire to a Knight Errant.

CHAPTER IX

How Sancho paid the Reckoning at the Inn which
Don Quixote supposed was a Castle

Now whilst Sancho Panza lay groaning in his bed, Don
Quixote, who, as we have said, felt somewhat eased and
cured, made up his mind to set off in search of new adventures. And full of this desire he himself saddled Rozinante and put the pack-saddle on his Squire's beast, and
helped Sancho to dress and to mount his Ass. Then
getting a-horseback he rode over to the corner of the
Inn and seized hold of a pike which stood there, to make
it serve him instead of a lance.

All the people that were staying at the Inn, some
twenty in number, stood staring at him, and among these
was the Innkeeper's daughter. Don Quixote kept turning his eyes towards her and sighing dolefully, which
every one, or at least all who had seen him the night before, thought must be caused by the pain he was in from
his bruises.

When they were both mounted and standing by the
Inn gate, he called to the Innkeeper and said in a grave
voice: 'Many and great are the favours, Sir Constable,
which I have received in this your Castle, and I shall remain deeply grateful for them all the days of my life. If

HOW SANCHO PAID
THE RECKONING

I am able to repay you by avenging you on some proud miscreant that hath done you any wrong, know that it is my office to help the weak, to revenge the wronged, and to punish traitors. Ransack your memory, and if you find anything of this sort for me to do, you have but to utter it, and I promise you, by the Order of Knighthood which I have received, to procure you satisfaction to your heart's content.'

'Sir Knight,' replied the Innkeeper with equal gravity, 'I have no need that your Worship should avenge me any wrong, for I know how to take what revenge I think good when an injury is done. All I want is that your Worship should pay me the score you have run up this night in mine Inn, both for the straw and barley of your two beasts, and your suppers and your beds.'

'This then is an Inn?' exclaimed Don Quixote.

'Ay, that it is, and a very respectable one, too,' replied the Innkeeper.

'All this time then I have been deceived,' said Don Quixote, 'for in truth I thought it was a Castle and no mean one. But since it is indeed an Inn and no Castle, all that can be done now is to ask you to forgive me any payment, for I cannot break the laws of Knights Errant, of whom I know for certain that they never paid for lodging or aught else in the Inns where they stayed. For the good entertainment that is given them is their due reward for the sufferings they endure, seeking adventures both day and night, winter and summer a-foot and a-horseback, in thirst and hunger, in heat and cold, being exposed to all the storms of heaven and the hardships of earth.'

'All that is no business of mine,' retorted the Inn-keeper. 'Pay me what you owe me, and keep your tales of Knights Errant for those who want them. My business is to earn my living.'

'You are a fool and a saucy fellow,' said Don Quixote angrily, and, spurring Rozinante and brandishing his lance, he swept out of the Inn yard before any one could stop him, and rode on a good distance without waiting to see if his Squire was following.

The Innkeeper, when he saw him go without paying, ran up to get his due from Sancho Panza, who also re-fused to pay, and said to him: 'Sir, seeing I am Squire to a Knight Errant, the same rule and reason for not paying at inns and taverns hold as good for me as for my Master.'

The Innkeeper grew angry at these words, and threat-ened that if he did not pay speedily he would get it from him in a way he would not like.

Sancho replied that by the Order of Knighthood which his Lord and Master had received, he would not pay a penny though it cost him his life.

But his bad fortune so managed it, that there hap-pened to be at the Inn at this time four wool-combers of Segovia, and three needlemakers of Cordova, and two neighbours from Seville, all merry fellows, very mis-chievous and playsome. And as if they were all moved with one idea, they came up to Sancho, and pulling him down off his Ass, one of them ran in for the Innkeeper's blanket, and they flung him into it. But looking up and seeing that the ceiling was somewhat lower than they needed for their business, they determined to go out into the yard, which had no roof but the sky, and there placing Sancho in the middle of the blanket, they began to toss him aloft and to make sport with him by throwing him up and down. The outcries of the miserable betossed Squire were so many and so loud that they reached the ears of his Master, who, standing awhile to listen what it was, believed that some new adventure was at hand, until he clearly recognised the shrieks to come from poor Sancho. Immediately turning his horse, he rode back at a gallop to the Inn gate, and finding it closed, rode round the wall to see if he could find any place at which he might enter. But he scarcely got to the wall of the Inn yard, which was not very high, when he beheld the wicked sport they were making with his Squire. He saw him go up and down with such grace and agility, that, had his anger allowed him, I make no doubt he would have burst with laughter. He tried to climb the wall from his horse, but he was so bruised and broken that he could by no means alight from his saddle, and therefore from on top of his horse he used such terrible threats against those that were tossing Sancho that one could not set them down in writing.

But in spite of his reproaches they did not cease from their laughter or labour, nor did the flying Sancho stop his lamentations, mingled now with threats and now with prayers. Thus they carried on their merry game, until at last from sheer weariness they stopped and let him be. And then they brought him his Ass, and, helping him to mount it, wrapped him in his coat, and the kind-hearted Maritornes, seeing him so exhausted, gave him a pitcher of water, which, that it might be the cooler, she fetched from the well.

Just as he was going to drink he heard his Master's voice calling to him, saying: 'Son Sancho, drink not water, drink it not, my son, for it will kill thee. Behold, here I have that most holy Balsam,'—and he showed him the can of liquor,—'two drops of which if thou drinkest thou wilt undoubtedly be cured.'

At these words Sancho shuddered, and replied to his Master: 'You forget surely that I am no Knight, or else you do not remember the pains I suffered last evening. Keep the liquor to yourself, and let me be in peace.'

At the conclusion of this speech he began to drink, but finding it was only water he would not taste it, and called for wine, which Maritornes very kindly fetched for him, and likewise paid for it out of her own purse.

As soon as Sancho had finished drinking, he stuck his heels into his Ass, and the Inn gate being thrown wide open he rode out, highly pleased at having paid for nothing, even at the price of a tossing. The Innkeeper, however, had kept his wallet, but Sancho was so distracted when he departed that he never missed it.

When Sancho reached his Master, he was almost too jaded and faint to ride his beast. Don Quixote, seeing him in this plight, said to him: 'Now I am certain that yon Castle or Inn is without doubt enchanted, for those who made sport with thee so cruelly, what else could they be but phantoms, and beings of another world?

And I am the more sure of this, because when I was by the wall of the Inn yard I was not able to mount it, or to alight from Rozinante, and therefore I must have been enchanted. For if I could have moved, I would have avenged thee in a way to make those scoundrels remember the jest for ever, even although to do it I should have had to disobey the rules of Knighthood.'

'So would I also have avenged myself,' said Sancho, 'Knight or no Knight, but I could not. And yet I believe that those who amused themselves with me were no phantoms or enchanted beings, but men of flesh and bones as we are, for one called Pedro, and another Tenorio, and the Innkeeper called a third Juan. But what I make out of all this, is that those adventures which we go in search of, will bring us at last so many misadventures that we shall not know our right foot from our left. And the best thing for us to do, in my humble opinion, is to return us again to our village and look after our own affairs, and not go jumping, as the saying is, "out of the frying-pan into the fire."'

'How little dost thou know of Knighthood, friend Sancho,' replied Don Quixote. 'Peace, and have patience, for a day will come when thou shalt see with thine own eyes how fine a thing it is to follow this calling. What pleasure can equal that of winning a battle or triumphing over an enemy?'

'I cannot tell,' answered Sancho; 'but this I know, that since we are Knights Errant, we have never won any battle unless it was that with the Biscayan, and even then your Worship lost half an ear. And ever after that time it has been nothing but cudgels and more cudgels, blows and more blows—I getting the tossing in the blanket to boot. And all this happens to me from enchanted people on whom I cannot take vengeance.'

'That grieves me,' replied Don Quixote; 'but who knows what may happen? Fortune may bring me a sword like that of Amadis, which did not only cut like a razor, but there was no armour however strong or enchanted which could stand before it.'

'It will be like my luck,' said Sancho, 'that when your Worship finds such a sword it will, like the Balsam, be of use only to those who are Knights, whilst poor Squires will still have to sup sorrow.'

'Fear not that, Sancho,' replied his Master; and he rode ahead, his mind full of adventures, followed at a little distance by his unhappy Squire.

OF THE ADVEN-
'TURE OF THE
TWO ARMIES·

CHAPTER X

Of the Adventure of the Two Armies

WHILST they were riding on their way, Don Quixote saw a large, dense cloud of dust rolling towards them, and turning to Sancho said: 'This is the day on which shall be shown the might of my arm and on which I am to do deeds which shall be written in the books of fame. Dost thou see the dust which arises there? Know then that it is caused by a mighty army composed of various and numberless nations that are marching this way.'

'If that be so,' replied Sancho, 'then must there be two armies, for on this other side there is as great a dust.'

Don Quixote turned round to behold it, and seeing that it was so, he was marvellous glad, for he imagined that there were indeed two armies coming to fight each other in the midst of that spacious plain. For at every hour and moment his fancy was full of battles, enchantments, and adventures, such as are related in the books of Knighthood, and all his thoughts and wishes were turned towards such things.

As for the clouds he had seen, they were raised by two large flocks of sheep which were being driven along the same road from two opposite sides, and this by reason of the dust could not be seen until they came near.

Don Quixote was so much in earnest when he called them armies that Sancho at once believed it, asking: 'What then shall we do, good Master?'

'What!' cried Don Quixote. 'Why, favour and help those who are in distress and need. Thou must know, Sancho, that this which comes on our front is led by the mighty Emperor Alifamfaron, Lord of the great Island of Trapobana. This other which is marching at our back is the army of his foe, the King of the Garamantes, Pentapolin of the Naked Arm, for he always goes into battle with his right arm bare.'

'But why do these two Princes hate each other so much?' asked Sancho.

'They are enemies,' replied Don Quixote, 'because Alifamfaron is a furious pagan and is deeply in love with Pantapolin's daughter, who is a beautiful and gracious Princess and a Christian. Her father refuses to give her to the pagan King until he abandons Mahomet's false religion and becomes a convert to his own.'

'By my beard,' said Sancho, 'Pentapolin does right well, and I will help him all I can.'

'Then thou wilt but do thy duty,' said Don Quixote, 'for it is not necessary to be a dubbed Knight to engage in battles such as these.'

'Right!' replied Sancho, 'but where shall we stow this Ass that we may be sure of finding him after the fight is over, for I think it is not the custom to enter into battle mounted on such a beast.'

'That is true,' said Don Quixote; 'but thou mayest safely leave it to chance whether he be lost or found, for after this battle we shall have so many horses that even Rozinante runs a risk of being changed for another. And now let us withdraw to that hillock yonder that we may get a better view of both those great armies.'

They did so, and standing on the top of a hill gazed at the two great clouds of dust which the imagination of Don Quixote had turned into armies. And then Don Quixote, with all the eloquence he could muster, described to Sancho the names of the different Knights in the two armies, with their colours and devices and mottoes, and the numbers of their squadrons, and the countries and provinces from which they came.

But though Sancho stood and listened in wonder he could see nothing as yet of Knights or armies, and at last he cried out: 'Where are all these grand Knights, good my Master? For myself, I can see none of them. But perhaps it is all enchantment, as so many things have been.'

'How! Sayest thou so?' said Don Quixote. 'Dost thou

not hear the horses neigh and the trumpets sound and the noise of the drums?'

'I hear nothing else,' said Sancho, 'but the great bleating of sheep.'

And so it was, indeed, for by this time the two flocks were approaching very near to them.

'The fear thou art in,' said Don Quixote, 'permits thee neither to see nor hear aright, for one of the effects of fear is to disturb the senses and make things seem different from what they are. If thou art afraid, stand to one side and leave me to myself, for I alone can give the victory to the side which I assist.'

So saying he clapped spurs to Rozinante, and, setting his lance in rest, rode down the hillside like a thunderbolt.

Sancho shouted after him as loud as he could: 'Return, good Sir Don Quixote! Return! For verily all those you go to charge are but sheep and muttons. Return, I say! Alas that ever I was born! What madness is this? Look, there are neither Knights nor arms, nor shields, nor soldiers, nor Emperors, but only sheep. What is it you do, wretch that I am?'

For all this Don Quixote did not turn back, but rode on, shouting in a loud voice: 'So ho! Knights! Ye that serve and fight under the banner of Pentapolin of the Naked Arm, follow me, all of you. Ye shall see how easily I will revenge him on his enemy Alifamfaron of Trapobana!'

With these words he dashed into the midst of the flock

of sheep, and began to spear them with as much courage and fury as if he were fighting his mortal enemies.

The Shepherds that came with the flock cried to him to leave off, but seeing their words had no effect they unloosed their slings and began to salute his pate with stones as big as one's fist.

But Don Quixote made no account of their stones, and galloping to and fro everywhere cried out: 'Where art thou, proud Alifamfaron? Where art thou? Come to me, for I am but one Knight alone, who desires to prove my strength with thee, man to man, and make thee yield thy life for the wrong thou hast done to the valorous Pentapolin.'

At that instant a stone gave him such a blow that it buried two of his ribs in his body. Finding himself so illtreated he thought for certain that he was killed or sorely wounded, and recollecting his Balsam, he drew out his oil pot and set it to his mouth to drink. But before he could take as much as he wanted, another stone struck him full on the hand, broke the oil pot into pieces, and carried away with it three or four teeth and grinders out of his mouth, and sorely crushed two fingers of his hand. So badly was he wounded by these two blows that he now fell off his horse on to the ground.

The Shepherds ran up, and believing that they had killed him, they collected their flocks in great haste, and carrying away their dead muttons, of which there were seven, they went away without caring to inquire into things any further.

Sancho was all this time standing on the hill looking at

the mad pranks his Master was performing, and tearing his beard and cursing the hour when they had first met. Seeing, however, that he was fallen on the ground, and the Shepherds had gone away, he came down the hill and went up to his Master, and found him in a very bad way, although not quite impossible.

'Did I not tell you, Sir Don Quixote,' said Sancho mournfully, 'did I not tell you to come back, for those you went to attack were not armies but sheep?'

'That thief of an Enchanter, my enemy, can alter things and make men vanish away as he pleases. Know, Sancho, that it is very easy for those kind of men to make us seem what they please, and this malicious being who persecutes me, envious of the glory that I was to reap from this battle, hath changed the Squadrons of the foe into flocks of sheep. If thou dost not believe me, Sancho, get on thine Ass and follow them fair and softly, and thou shalt see that when they have gone a little way off they will return to their original shapes, and, ceasing to be sheep, become men as right and straight as I painted them to you at first.'

At this moment the Balsam that Don Quixote had swallowed began to make him very sick, and Sancho Panza ran off to search in his wallet for something that might cure him. But when he found that his wallet was not upon his Ass, and remembered for the first time that it was left at the Inn, he was on the point of losing his wits. He cursed himself anew, and resolved in his heart to leave his Master and return to his house, even though he should lose his wages and the government of the promised Island.

Don Quixote had now risen, and with his left hand to his mouth that the rest of his teeth might not fall out, with the other he took Rozinante by the bridle, and went up to where his Squire stood leaning against his Ass with his head in his hand, looking the picture of misery.

Don Quixote, seeing him look so miserable, said to him: 'Learn, Sancho, not to be so easily downcast, for these storms that befall us are signs that the weather will soon be fair. Therefore thou shouldst not vex thyself about my misfortunes, for sure thou dost not share in them.'

'How not?' replied Sancho; 'mayhap he they tossed in a blanket yesterday was not my father's son? And the wallet which is missing to-day with all my chattels is not that my misfortune?'

'What, is the wallet missing, Sancho?' said Don Quixote.

'Yes, it is missing,' answered Sancho.

'In that case we have nothing to eat to-day,' said Don Quixote.

'It would be so,' said Sancho, 'should the herbs of the field fail us, which your Worship says you know of, and with which you have told me Knights Errant must supply their wants.'

'Nevertheless,' answered Don Quixote, 'I would rather just now have a hunch of bread, or a cottage loaf and a couple of pilchards' heads, than all the herbs that Dioscorides has described. But before thou mountest thine

Ass, lend me here thy hand and see how many teeth and grinders are lacking on this right side of my upper jaw, for there I feel the pain.'

Sancho put his fingers in, and, feeling about, asked: 'How many grinders did your Worship have before, on this side?'

'Four,' replied Don Quixote, 'besides the wisdom tooth, all whole and sound.'

'Mind well what you say, Sir,' answered Sancho.

'Four, say I, if not five,' said Don Quixote, 'for in all my life I never had tooth or grinder drawn from my mouth, nor has any fallen out or been destroyed by decay.'

'Well, then, in this lower part,' said Sancho, 'your Worship has but two grinders and a half, and in the upper, neither a half nor any, for all is as smooth as the palm of my hand.'

'Unfortunate I!' exclaimed Don Quixote, 'for I would rather they had deprived me of my arm, as long as it were not my sword arm. Know, Sancho, that a mouth without grinders is like a mill without a grindstone, and a tooth is more to be prized that a millstone. But all this must we suffer who profess the stern rule of Knights Errant. Mount, friend, and lead the way, for I will follow thee what pace thou pleasest.'

OF A WONDERFUL
ADVENTURE —

CHAPTER XI

Of a wonderful Adventure which Don Quixote
went through without peril to himself or
Sancho

'Methinks, my Master,' said Sancho, 'that all the mishaps
that have befallen us in these days are without doubt in
punishment for the sin you committed against the rules
of Knighthood, in not keeping your vow which you
made, not to eat bread, and all the other things you
vowed to do, until you got the helmet of Malandrino, or
whatever his name was.'

'Thou are very right, Sancho,' said Don Quixote; 'but
to tell the truth it had passed from my memory; but I

will make amends as may be done by the rules of Knighthood.'

'And doubtless,' replied Sancho, 'all will then be well, and I shall live to see none so great as Don Quixote of the Mancha, the Knight of the Rueful Countenance.'

'Why do you give me that name, good Sancho?' asked his Master.

'Because truly,' replied his Squire, 'your Worship has now the most ill-favoured face that any man ever saw, and it must be, I think, because you are tired out after the battle, or on account of the loss of your grinders.'

'I fancy,' said Don Quixote, 'that some sage must have put it into thy head to give me such a name, for now I remember that all Knights took a name of that kind, and there was "The Knight of the Flaming Sword," and "The Knight of the Griffin," and many another. And from this day forward I shall call myself by no other name than "The Knight of the Rueful Countenance"; and that the name may become me better, I will upon the first occasion cause to be painted on my shield a most ill-favoured and sorrowful face.'

'There is no need,' said Sancho, 'to waste time and money in having the countenance painted. All that has to be done is that your Worship should discover your own, and show your face to those that look at you, when without doubt they will name you "He of the Rueful Countenance." Hunger and the loss of teeth have given your Worship so evil a face that you may spare yourself the painting.'

Don Quixote laughed at his Squire's pleasantry, but

determined nevertheless to have the painting made on his shield according to his fancy.

They had now arrived at a wide but hidden valley between two mountains, where they alighted; and seeing a meadow on the side of the hill thick with green and tender grass, they entered it and marched along, feeling their way, for the night was so dark they could not see a jot.

They had scarcely gone two hundred paces when they heard a great noise of water, as if it fell headlong from some great and steep rock, and being by this time very thirsty, the sound cheered them greatly.

Stopping to listen whence it came, they heard another loud noise, which drowned all their joy, especially Sancho's, who, as I have said, was by nature timid and easily frightened.

They heard, I say, certain blows, louder than the sound of the rushing water, and struck in regular beats, accompanied by the ugly sounds of rattling irons and chains. These, with the furious sounds of the water, and the surrounding darkness, were enough to strike terror into any heart less brave than Don Quixote's.

The night, as I said, was dark, and they were now among some tall trees, whose leaves, moved by a gentle breeze, made a low whispering sound, so that the loneliness of the place, the darkness, the noise of the water, the strange sounds of the heavy beating and rattling chains, all caused horror and fright, the more so when they found that the blows never ceased, and morning seemed as though it would never come.

But Don Quixote was not disturbed by these things, and leaping on Rozinante, he seized his shield, brandished his lance, and said: 'Friend Sancho, I am he for whom are reserved all dangerous, great, and valorous feats. I am he who shall cause the feats of the Knights of the Round Table to be forgotten. Mark well, trusty and loyal Squire, the darkness of this night, the strange stillness, the dull, confused trembling of the leaves, the dreadful noise of the water, which seems as though it were leaping down from the steep mountains of the moon, the constant thumping of the blows which wounds and pains our ears, which all together and each by itself are enough to strike terror, fear, and amazement into the mind of Mars, how much more in his that is not accustomed to such adventures. But with me it causeth my heart to almost burst in my bosom with joy to try this peril, however great it may be. Therefore tighten Rozinante's girths a little, and may all be well with thee. Wait for me here three days and no more. And if I do not return in the end of that time, go back to our village, and from thence, for my sake, to Toboso, where thou shalt say to my incomparable Lady Dulcinea that her captive Knight died attempting things that might make him worthy to be called hers.'

When Sancho heard his Master say these things he began to weep piteously, and said to him: 'Sir, I see no reason why you should undertake this fearful adventure. It is now night, there is no one sees us, we can easily turn aside and go away from the danger, and since no one can set us down as cowards. Remember that I left my country, wife, and children to come and serve you, and to obtain that unlucky and accursed Island you have promised me so often, and now you mean to forsake me here in this desert. Put it off at least until the morning, for it can want but little from this to daybreak.'

'Let it want what it may,' answered Don Quixote, 'it shall never be said of me that tears or prayers hindered my doing my duty as a Knight.'

Sancho, seeing that his Master's mind was made up, and that his tears, entreaties, and prayers were of no avail, determined to use his wits, and see if by trickery he could make him wait until daybreak. And so, when he was tightening the horse's girths, he softly and without being felt tied his Ass's halter to both Rozinante's legs, so fast that when Don Quixote thought to depart he could not, for his horse was not able to go a step except by little jumps.

Sancho, seeing the success of his trick, exclaimed: 'Behold, Sir, how Heaven, moved by my tears and prayers, has ruled that Rozinante shall not be able to go a step; and if you persist in urging, spurring, and striking him, it will be to anger Fortune, and kick, as the saying is, against the pricks.'

Don Quixote grew angry at this, and yet the more he spurred Rozinante the less would he move. But at last he became convinced that it was no further use attempting to make him go, and resolved to remain quiet until the morning came, or until Rozinante would please to depart. And having no idea that Sancho was the cause of this, he said to him: 'Since it is so, Sancho, that Rozinante is not able to move, I am content to wait here until morning smiles, although I weep to think it may be so long in coming.'

'You shall have no cause to weep,' replied Sancho; 'for I will tell you stories from now till daylight, unless you would like to dismount and snatch a little sleep upon the green grass, after the custom of Knights Errant, that you may be the fresher the morrow to finish this terrible adventure.'

'Who talks of sleeping?' said Don Quixote angrily. 'Am I one of those Knights that repose in time of danger? Sleep thou, who wast born to sleep, or do what thou please, for I shall do what I think right.'

'Good Sir, be not angry,' said Sancho, 'for I did not mean that'; and coming as near to his Master as he durst, he placed one hand on the pommel of his saddle and crept as near as he could, so great was the fear he had of those blows, which all the while did sound without ceasing.

After many hours spent in conversation the dawn approached, and Sancho, seeing this, unloosed Rozinante very carefully. As soon as the horse felt himself free, though he was never very mettlesome, he began to paw with his hoofs, and Don Quixote, noticing that he moved, took it for a good sign, and believed that it was now time to attempt this fearful adventure.

And now the sun had risen, and everything appeared distinctly, and Don Quixote saw that he was among some tall chestnut-trees that cast a very dark shadow. He perceived that the hammering did not cease, but could not

discover what caused it, and so without delay he spurred
Rozinante, and turning back again to Sancho to bid him
farewell, commanded him to stay for him there three
days at the longest, and that if he returned not then, to
take it for certain that he had ended his days in that peril-
ous adventure. He again repeated to him the message
which he had to carry to Lady Dulcinea, and assured
him that if he came safe out of this dreadful peril, the
Squire might hold the promised Island as more than certain.

Here Sancho began to weep afresh at the pitiful words
of his good Master, and determined not to abandon him
until the last end of this adventure. And thereupon Don
Quixote rode forward towards the terrible noises, Sancho
following him on foot, leading by the halter his good
Dapple, who was the constant companion of his good or
evil fortune.

Having gone a good distance among those chestnuts
and shady trees, they came to a little meadow which lay
at the foot of some high rocks, down which a mighty rush
of water descended. At the foot of the rocks were some
houses, so roughly built that they seemed more like ruins
than houses, from whence came the din and clatter of
the strokes which still never ceased.

Rozinante started at the noise of the water and the
hammering, and being made quiet by Don Quixote, drew
near little by little to the houses. Don Quixote murmured devoutly the name of his beloved Lady Dulcinea,
and Sancho, never apart from his Master's side, stretched
out his neck and eyes as far as he could, to see if he could

make out what it was that caused them so much terror and dismay.

And when they had gone about another hundred paces they turned a corner, and there before their eyes was the cause of that hideous and terrible noise that had kept them all the night so miserable and frightened. This was nothing worse than a mill for fulling cloth, whose six great iron maces or pestles, driven by the water-wheels, kept on day and night falling and rising from their troughs with successive hammering blows. And this had caused the terrible noise which had so terrified the adventurers.

When Don Quixote saw what it was, he stood mute and ashamed. Sancho beheld him, and saw that he hung his head on his breast. Don Quixote looked also at his Squire, and saw that his cheeks were swollen with laughter, with evident signs that he was in danger of bursting. Don Quixote's melancholy was not so great that he could help smiling a little at seeing Sancho, and Sancho, when he saw his Master beginning to laugh, burst out loud and long, with such force that he had to put his hands to his sides to prevent them splitting.

Four times he ended and four times he started again; but what chiefly enraged Don Quixote was that he began to repeat in a jesting manner, imitating his Master: 'Friend Sancho, I am he for whom are reserved all dangerous, great, and valorous feats.' And he went on repeating the greater part of what Don Quixote had said when they first heard the fearsome sounds.

This was more than Don Quixote could bear, and lifting up the end of his lance, he gave him two such blows on the back, that if he had caught them on his pate they would have freed his Master from paying him any more wages.

Sancho, seeing that he had carried the jest too far, said very humbly: 'Please, good Master, I did but jest.'

'But why dost thou jest? I tell thee I do not jest,' replied Don Quixote. 'Come here, Master Merryman, and tell me, am I, being as I am a Knight, to distinguish noises, and to know which are those of mills and which are of Giants? Turn me those six hammers into Giants and cast them at me, one by one, or all together, and if I do not turn all their heels up, then mock me as much as thou pleasest.'

'No more, good Sir,' said Sancho, 'for I confess I have been somewhat too laughsome, but henceforth you may be sure that I will not once unfold my lips to jest at your doings, but only to honour you as my Master and Lord.'

'By doing so thou shalt live on the face of the earth, for next to our parents we are bound to respect our Masters as if they were our fathers.'

CHAPTER XII

The great Adventure and rich Winning of the
Helmet of Mambrino

IT now began to rain, and Sancho would have entered one of the fulling-mills for shelter, but Don Quixote had taken such a dislike to them, on account of the jest of which he had been the victim, that he would not go near them.

Turning to the right, he made away into a highroad not unlike the one on which they had travelled the day before. Very shortly Don Quixote espied a man a-horseback who wore on his head something that glittered like gold. Scarce had he seen him when he turned to Sancho and said: 'Methinks, Sancho, that there is no proverb that is not true, for all proverbs are sentences taken out of experience itself, which is the universal mother of all sciences. And there is a proverb which says, "When one door shuts another opens." I say this because if Fortune closed the door for us last night, deceiving us in the adventure of the fulling-mills, to-day it opens wide the door to a better and more certain adventure. For here, if I be not deceived, there comes one towards us that wears on

THE RICH WINNING OF
THE HELMET OF MAMBRINO

his head the helmet of Mambrino, about which I made the oath thou knowest of.'

'See well what you say, Sir, and better what you do,' said Sancho, 'for I would not meet with more fulling-mills to hammer us out of our senses.'

'Peace, fellow!' cried Don Quixote; 'what has a helmet to do with fulling-mills?'

'I know not,' replied Sancho; 'but if I might speak as I used to, I would give you such reasons that your Worship should see that you were mistaken in what you say.'

'How can I be mistaken in what I say?' cried Don Quixote. 'Tell me, seest thou not that Knight who comes riding towards us on a dapple grey horse, with a helmet of gold on his head?'

'That which I see and make out,' replied Sancho, 'is nothing but a man on a grey ass like mine carrying on his head something which shines.'

'Why that is Mambrino's helmet,' said Don Quixote. 'Stand aside and leave me alone with him, and thou shalt see how, without a word, this adventure shall be ended and the helmet I have longed for be mine.'

'As to standing aside,' muttered Sancho, 'that I will take care to do, but I trust this is not another case of fulling-mills.'

'I have already told thee,' said Don Quixote angrily, 'to make no mention of the mills, and if thou dost not obey me, I vow that I will batter the soul out of thy body.'

At this Sancho, fearing lest his Master should carry out his threat, held his peace.

Now the truth of the matter as to the helmet, the horse, and the Knight which Don Quixote saw, was this. There were in that neighbourhood two villages, the one so small that it had neither shop nor barber, but the larger one had; and the barber, therefore, served the smaller village on any occasion when any one wanted his beard trimmed.

It so happened that he was now journeying to the smaller village, bringing with him a brazen basin, and as he rode along it chanced to rain, and therefore, to save his hat, which was a new one, he clapped the basin on his head, and the basin being clean scoured, glittered half a league off. He rode upon a grey ass, as Sancho said, and that was the reason why Don Quixote took him to be a Knight with a helmet of gold riding on a dapple grey steed, for everything he came across he made to fit in with the things he had read of in the books of Knighthood.

And when he saw the unfortunate rider draw near, without stopping to speak a word, he ran at him with his lance, putting Rozinante at full gallop, and intending to pierce him through and through. And as he came up to him, without stopping his horse, he shouted to him: 'Defend thyself, caitiff wretch, or else render to me of thine own will what is mine by all the rights of war.'

The barber, who saw this wild figure bearing down on him as he was riding along without thought or fear of attack, had no other way to avoid the thrust of the lance than to fall off his ass on to the ground. And no sooner did he touch the earth than he sprang up more nimbly than a deer and raced away across the plain faster than the wind, leaving behind him on the ground the coveted basin. With this Don Quixote was well content, and said that the Pagan was a wise man in leaving behind him that for which he was attacked.

Then he commended Sancho to take up the helmet, who lifting it said: 'The basin is a good one, and is worth eight *reals* if it is worth a farthing.'

He gave it to his Master, who placed it upon his head, turning it about from side to side in search of the visor, and seeing he could not find it, said: 'Doubtless the Pagan for whom this helmet was first forged had a very great head, and the worst of it is that half of the helmet is wanting.'

When Sancho heard him call the basin a helmet he could not contain his laughter, but presently remembering his Master's anger, he checked himself in the midst of it.

'Why dost thou laugh, Sancho?' said Don Quixote. 'I laugh,' said he, 'to think of the great head the Pagan owner of this helmet had. For it is all the world like a barber's basin.'

'Know, Sancho, that I imagine,' replied Don Quixote, 'that this famous piece of the enchanted helmet must by some strange accident have fallen into someone's hands that knew not its great worth, and seeing that it was of pure gold, he hath melted down one half and made of the other half this, which seems, as thou sayest, to be a barber's basin. But be that as it may, to me, who know its value, its transformation makes no matter. I will have it altered at the first village where I can find a smith, and meanwhile I will wear it as well as I can, for something is better than nothing, all the more as it will do to protect me against any blow from a stone.'

'That is,' said Sancho, 'if they do not shoot from a sling, as they shot in the battle of the two armies, when they made their mark on your Worship's grinders and broke the oil-pot wherein you carried that blessed Balsam.'

'I do not much care for the loss of the Balsam,' replied Don Quixote, 'for as thou knowest, Sancho, I have the receipt for it in my memory.'

'So have I too,' groaned Sancho; 'but if ever I make it or try it again as long as I live may this be my last hour. But letting that pass, what shall we do with this dapple grey steed that looks so like a grey ass, that Martino, or whatever his name was, has left behind him? For from the haste he made to get away I do not think he intends to come back, and by my beard the beast is a good one.'

'I am not accustomed to ransack and spoil those whom I overcome, nor is it the practice of Knighthood to take the horses of others unless the victor chance in combat to lose his own. Therefore Sancho, leave the horse or ass, or what else thou pleasest to call it, for when his owner sees us depart he will return again for it.'

'Truly,' said Sancho, 'the laws of Knighthood are strict, and if I may not change one ass for another, may I at least change the harness?'

'Of that I am not very sure,' said Don Quixote, 'and as it is a matter of doubt, you must not change them unless thy need is extreme.'

'So extreme,' said Sancho, 'that if they were for mine own person I could not need them more.'

So saying he decked out his Ass with a thousand fineries robbed from the other, and made him look vastly better. Then, having taken a drink at the stream, they turned their backs on the hateful fulling-mills, and rode along the highroad, Don Quixote all the way describing to Sancho the successes in store for them, until he was interrupted by an adventure that must be told in another chapter.

DON QUIXOTE
FREES THE
GALLEY SLAVES

CHAPTER XIII

How Don Quixote set at liberty many poor
Wretches who were being taken to a Place
to which they had no wish to go

As they rode onwards, Don Quixote lifted up his eyes
and saw coming along the road about a dozen men on
foot, strung together on a great wire chain like beads.
The chain was fastened round their necks, and they had
manacles on their hands. There rode with them two men
a-horseback, and two others followed on foot. The horsemen had firelocks, and those on foot javelins and swords.

As soon as Sancho saw them he said: 'This is a chain

of galley slaves, people forced by the King to go to the galleys.'

'How! People forced?' asked Don Quixote. 'Is it possible that the King will force anybody?'

'I say not so,' answered Sancho, 'but they are people condemned for their offences to serve the King in the galleys.'

'In fact,' replied Don Quixote, 'however you put it, these folk are being taken where they go by force and not of their own free will.'

'That is so,' said Sancho.

'Then if it be so,' continued his Master, 'here I see before me my duty to redress outrages and to give help to the poor and the afflicted.'

'I pray you, Sir,' said Sancho, 'consider that Justice, representing the King himself, does wrong or violence to nobody, but only punishes those who have committed crimes.'

By this time the chain of galley slaves came up, and Don Quixote in very courteous words asked those in charge of them to be good enough to inform him why they carried people away in that manner.

One of the guardians a-horseback answered that they were slaves condemned by his Majesty to the galleys, and that there was no more to be said, nor ought Don Quixote to desire any further information.

'For all that,' replied Don Quixote very politely, 'I would fain learn from every one of them the cause of his disgrace.'

To this the guardian a-horseback answered: 'Although

we carry here the register of the crimes of all these wretches, yet if you wish to do so, ask it from themselves; and no doubt they will tell you their stories, for they are men who take delight in boasting of their rascalities.'

With this permission, which Don Quixote would have taken for himself if they had not given it, he went up to the chain and asked of the first one for what sins he had found himself in such straits.

He answered that his offence was no other than for being in love.

'For that and no more?' cried Don Quixote; 'but if folk are sent there for being in love, I should have been pulling an oar there long ago.'

'My love was not of the kind your Worship imagines,' replied the galley slave, 'for mine was that I loved overmuch a basket stuffed with fine linen, which I embraced so lovingly, that if the law had not taken it from me by violence, I should not of my own free will have forsaken it till now. I was taken in the act and sent for three years to the galleys.'

Don Quixote now inquired of the second his cause of offence, but he answered him not a word, seeming too downcast and melancholy to speak. But the first one spoke for him, and said: 'Sir, this man goes for being a Canary bird—I mean a musician or singer.'

'Is it possible,' said Don Quixote, 'that musicians and singers are sent to the galleys?'

'Yes, indeed,' said the slave, 'there is nothing worse than to sing in anguish.'

'I do not understand it,' said Don Quixote, 'but I have heard say that he who sings scares away sorrow.'

But one of the guards interrupted him and said: 'Sir Knight, among these wretches "to sing in anguish" means to confess on the rack. They put this poor wretch to the torture, and he confessed that he was a stealer of beasts. And because he has confessed he is condemned to the galleys for six years. And he is sad and pensive because the other thieves maltreat, abuse, and despise him. For, as they say, a *nay* has as many letters as a *yea*, and it is good luck for a criminal when there are no witnesses and proofs, and his fate depends on his own tongue, and in my opinion there is much reason in that.'

'I think so likewise,' said Don Quixote, and he passed on to where the third slave stood, and put to him the same question as to the others.

The man replied very coolly, saying: 'I go to the galleys because I wanted ten ducats.'

'I will give thee twenty with all my heart to free thee from that misfortune,' said Don Quixote.

'That,' replied the Slave, 'would be like one that hath money in the midst of the sea, and yet is dying of hunger because he can get no meat to buy with it. If I had had the twenty ducats your Worship offers me at the right time, I would have greased the lawyer's pen with them, and so sharpened the advocate's wit, that instead of being trailed along here like a greyhound, I should now have been walking about in the market-place of Toledo. What must be must be!'

Don Quixote went from one to another, receiving different answers, until he came to the last, who was a man about thirty years old, of very comely looks, except that he had a squint. He was differently tied from the rest, for he wore a chain to his leg, so long that it wound round his whole body. He had besides round his neck two iron rings, from one of which two wires came down to his waist on which were fastened two manacles. These held his hands fast locked with a great hanging lock, so that he could neither put his hand to his mouth nor bend down his head to his hands.

Don Quixote asked why he was so loaded with iron more than the rest.

The Guard answered that it was because he had committed more crimes than all the rest put together, and that he was such a desperate scoundrel that although they carried him tied up in that fashion, they were not sure of him, but feared that he might make an escape. 'He goes,' continued the Guard, 'to the galleys for ten years; and when I tell you he is the infamous Gines of Passamonte, you will need, I think, to know no more about him.'

At this, Gines, who seemed very impatient at the Guard's history, broke out into a torrent of abuse, and then, turning to Don Quixote, said: 'Sir Knight, if you have anything to bestow on us, give it us now, and be-gone, for you do but weary us by wanting to know the stories of other men's lives; and if you want to learn more, know that I am Gines of Passamonte, whose life has been written by his own hand.'

'He speaks truly,' said the Guard, 'for he himself hath penned his own history.'

'And how is the book called?' asked Don Quixote.

'It is called the *Life of Gines of Passamonte*,' replied the Slave.

'And is it yet ended?' inquired the Knight.

'How can it be finished,' replied Gines, 'seeing my life is not yet finished? I intend to finish it in the galleys.'

'You seem to be a clever fellow,' said Don Quixote.

'And an unlucky one,' replied Gines, 'for bad luck always pursues genius.'

'It pursues knaves,' interrupted the Guard; and at this Gines burst out again into abuse and bad language, which ended in the Guard threatening to beat him with his rod if he did not hold his peace.

At this Don Quixote put himself between them, and entreated the Guard not to use him hardly, seeing that it was not much that one who carried his hands so tied should have his tongue free.

Then turning himself towards the slaves he said: 'I have gathered from all you have said, dear brethren, that although they punish you for your faults, yet the pains you suffer do not please you, and that you march towards them with a very ill will. All this prompts me to do that for you, for which I was sent into the world, and for which I became a Knight Errant, and to which end I vowed at all times to succour the poor and help those that are oppressed. But as it is prudent not to do by foul means what can be done by fair, I will entreat these gentlemen your guardians that they will unloose you and let you depart in peace, for it seems to me a harsh thing to make slaves of those who are born free.' And turning to the guards he continued: 'These things I ask of you in a peaceable and quiet manner, and if you grant my request I shall give you my thanks; but if you will not do it willingly, then shall this lance and sword of mine, guided by the invincible valour of mine arm, force you to do my will.'

'This is pretty fooling,' replied the Guard. 'Would you have us release to you those the King has imprisoned? Go your way, good Sir, settle the basin on your head more straightly, and study to find out, if you have wits enough, how many feet a cat has.'

'You are a cat and a rat and a knave!' said Don Quixote in a rage. And without a word he set on him so fiercely, and without giving him time to defend himself, that he struck him to the earth badly wounded with his lance. Luckily for the Knight this was the Guard that had the firelock.

At first the other guards stood astounded at this unexpected event. Then they recovered themselves, and the horsemen drew their swords, the footmen grasped their javelins, and all of them attacked Don Quixote, who quietly prepared to receive them. No doubt he would have been in some danger, but the slaves, seeing a chance of liberty, broke the chain by which they were linked together. The hurly-burly was such that the guards first ran to prevent the slaves getting free, then to defend themselves from Don Quixote who attacked them, so that they could do nothing to any purpose to keep their prisoners. Sancho, for his part, helped to loose Gines of Passamonte, who was the first to leap into the field free from all fetters, and setting upon the other overthrown guard, he took his sword and firelock from him. With the latter in his hand, by pointing it at one and aiming it at the other, he cleared the field of all the guards, who were the more easily got rid of because the galley slaves were now all at liberty, and showered at their late keepers volleys of stones.

When their victory was complete, Don Quixote called all the slaves together, and they gathered round to hear what he commanded, when he spoke to them as follows: 'It is the duty of well-bred people to be grateful for benefits received, and ingratitude is one of the worst of sins. I say this, Sirs, because you know what good you have received at my hand, and the only reward I ask is that you all go from here laden with the chains from which I have just freed your necks to the City of Toboso, and there present yourselves before the Lady Dulcinea of Toboso, and tell her that her Knight of the Rueful Countenance sends you there to do her service. Relate unto her the way in which I won your freedom; and this being done, you may then go your ways.'

Gines answered for all the rest, saying: 'That which you demand is impossible to perform, because we must not travel the roads together, but go alone and divided, to the end that we be not captured again by the guards of the Holy Brotherhood, who will make search for us. To tell us to go to Toboso is as absurd as to seek for pears on an elm-tree, and we shall not do it.'

At this Don Quixote was mightily enraged, and said: 'I tell thee, Don Gines, or whatever thy name is, that after what thou hast said thou shalt go thyself alone, with thy tail between thy legs and bearing the whole length of the chains with thee.'

Gines, who was a violent fellow, and quite understood that Don Quixote was not very wise, seeing the foolish way in which he had set them at liberty, would not stand this abuse, and winked at his companions, who, stepping aside, sent such a shower of stones against Don Quixote that he had not time to cover himself with his shield, and poor Rozinante was in such terror that he would not move forward to the attack. Sancho ran behind his Ass, and by this means sheltered himself from the tempest of stones that rained on both of them. Several stones struck Don Quixote on the body with such force that at last he fell from his horse and on to the ground, and no sooner was he fallen than Gines leaped upon him, and taking the basin from his head, gave him three or four blows with it on the shoulders, and afterwards struck it on the ground so as to break it into pieces. They then stripped him of a tunic he wore over his armour, and would have taken his stockings if they could have got them from under his armour. From Sancho they took his coat, leaving him in his shirt sleeves, and, dividing the spoils of battle among themselves, they made the best of their way off, each one as it pleased him, with no further thought of their benefactor or his Lady Dulcinea of Toboso.

The Ass, Rozinante, Sancho, and Don Quixote remained alone. The Ass, with drooping head, stood shaking his ears every now and then as if he thought the storm of stones was not yet over, Rozinante lay overthrown by his Master, who was lying on the ground, Sancho stood trembling at the thought of the bullets of the Holy Brotherhood, and Don Quixote was amazed to see himself so wickedly used by those to whom he had done so great a service.

CHAPTER XIV

Of what befell Don Quixote in the
Brown Mountains

Don Quixote, finding himself in such a bad plight, said to his Squire: 'I have often heard it said that to do good to ungrateful men is to cast water into the sea. If I had listened to your advice, I might have avoided this trouble. But, now that it is over, there is nothing for it but to be patient and to be wise another time.'

'If you take warning by this or anything else,' replied Sancho, 'call me a Turk. But, as you say, you might have avoided this trouble by taking my advice. Listen to what I say now, and you will avoid a greater danger. For let me tell you that it is no use talking about Knighthood and its customs to the Holy Brotherhood, for it cares not two farthings for all the Knights Errant in the world, and for myself. I seem to hear their arrows buzzing round my ears already.'

'Thou art by nature a coward, Sancho,' replied Don Quixote; 'but that thou mayest not say that I am obstinate, and that I never follow thine advice, I will take thy counsel this time, and hide myself from the attacks thou fearest so greatly. But it must be on one condition, that thou never tell to any mortal creature that I with-

DON QUIXOTE
MEETING CARDENIO

drew myself out of this danger for fear, but only to humour thy wishes. For if thou sayest anything else thou liest.'

'Sir,' answered Sancho Panza, 'to retreat is not to run away, nor is it wise to wait where there is more danger than hope, and it is the part of a wise man to spend to-day in keeping himself safe for to-morrow. Therefore, rude clown as I am, take my advice, and mount Rozinante and follow me as quickly as you are able.'

Don Quixote mounted Rozinante without another word, and, Sancho leading the way on his Ass, they entered that part of the Brown Mountains that was near them, a favourite haunt for outlaws and robbers in those days, and a spot where they would be safe from pursuit. For it was Sancho's plan to hide themselves for some days among the crags, so as not to be found even if the Holy Brotherhood should come and look for them.

They arrived that night in the very midst of the mountains, and there Sancho thought it best to spend the night, and, indeed, as many days as their food lasted; and with this intention they took up their abode among a number of tall trees that grew between two rocks.

It happened, however, that Gines of Passamonte, the famous cheat and robber whom Don Quixote by his valour and folly had released from his chains, resolved to hide himself also among the same mountains, and destiny led him to the very spot where Don Quixote and his Squire were hiding, and at the very moment that they had fallen asleep, tired out with the day's toil. And as the wicked are always ungrateful, and necessity forces them to evil deeds, Gines, who was neither grateful nor good natured, resolved to rob Sancho Panza of his Ass, not caring for Rozinante, as he thought he was not worth riding or selling. Sancho Panza slept soundly, and, while he slept, Gines stole his Ass, and before morning he was so far off as to be past finding.

The morning sun arose bringing joy to the earth, but only grief to poor Sancho, for he missed his Dapple, and, finding himself deprived of him, he began the saddest and most doleful lamentation possible, and when Don Quixote awoke he heard him mourning in a most melancholy way, crying out: 'O my beloved Ass, born in mine own house, the sport of my children, the comfort of my wife, the envy of my neighbours, the ease of my burdens, and, beyond all, the support of my household, for with what I gained daily by thee did I pay half of mine expenses!'

Don Quixote, who heard this lament, and knew the cause of it, comforted Sancho as best he could, and desired him to have patience, promising to give him a letter to command those at his house to hand over to him three out of five ass foals that he had at home. Sancho was comforted by this, dried his tears, moderated his sobs, and thanked Don Quixote for the favours he had done him.

And as they entered farther among the mountains the Knight felt glad at heart that he had come to a place so suitable for the adventures he was in search of. They reminded him of marvellous stories he had read of what had happened to Knights Errant in similar wild places, and his mind was so full of these things that he thought of nothing else whatever. As for Sancho, he trudged behind his Master, loaded with the things that his Ass should have carried.

While Sancho was thus walking along, he raised his eyes and saw that his Master had come to a stop, and was trying with the point of his lance to lift what seemed like a bundle that was lying on the ground. Upon which he ran to see whether his Master wanted his aid, and came up to him just as he was lifting up a saddle cushion with a portmanteau fast to it. These were half rotten and falling to pieces, yet they weighed so much that Sancho's help was required to lift them up. His Master ordered him to see what was in the portmanteau, and Sancho obeyed him as quickly as might be. And although it was shut with a chain and a padlock, yet Sancho could see through the rents and tears what was inside it, namely, four fine Holland shirts and other linen clothes, both curious and delicate, besides a handkerchief containing a good quantity of gold.

'At last,' cried Sancho, 'we have met with an adventure worth something,' and searching on he came across a little memorandum book very richly bound.

Don Quixote asked him for this, but bade him keep the money for himself.

For this rich favour Sancho kissed his hands, and taking all the linen, he crammed it into their provision-bag.

Don Quixote, having considered awhile, said: 'Methinks, Sancho, that some traveller having lost his way must have passed over the mountains, and being met by thieves, they slew him and buried him in this secret place.'

'It cannot be so,' answered Sancho, 'for if they had been thieves they would not have left the money behind them.'

'Thou sayest true,' said Don Quixote, 'and therefore I cannot guess what can have happened. But stay, we will look at the pocket-book, and see whether there is anything written in it by which we may discover what we want to know.'

He opened it, and the first thing he found in it was a poem, which was all about the author's love for some fair Chloe who would not care for him. Don Quixote read this aloud to Sancho.

'Nothing can be learned from these verses,' said the Squire, 'unless by that clue which is there we may get some help.'

'What clue is there here?' said Don Quixote.

'I thought your Lordship mentioned a clue there.'

'I did not say *clue*, but *Chloe*,' replied Don Quixote, 'which no doubt is the name of the lady of whom the author of this poem complains.'

After looking through the book again, Don Quixote found a despairing love-letter, and several other verses and letters full of laments and misery, from which he came to the conclusion that the owner of the book was some sad rejected lover.

The Knight of the Rueful Countenance was very desirous to know who was the owner of the portmanteau, believing from what he had seen that he must be a man of some position, whom the disdain and cruelty of a fair lady had driven to desperate courses. But as there was no one in this remote and solitary place to satisfy his curiosity, he rode on, taking any road that Rozinante chose, in the firm belief that he would find some strange adventure among the mountains.

And as he rode he saw a man on top of a little mountain, leaping from rock to rock and tuft to tuft with marvellous agility. He made him out to be half-naked, with a black and matted beard, his hair long and tangled, his feet unshod, and his legs bare. He wore some breeches of tawny velvet, but these appeared so torn to rags that his skin showed in many places. His head, too, was bare, and although he ran by with all haste, yet was the Knight able to mark all these things. But he could not follow him, because it was not in Rozinante's power, being in a weak state and naturally very slow and steady-going, to travel over these rough places at any speed. Don Quixote at once came to the conclusion that he was the owner of the portmanteau, and resolved to go in search of him, even if he should have to spend a whole year in the mountains till he found him. So he commanded Sancho to go on one side of the mountain, while he went the other, 'and,' said he, 'one of us may thus come across this man who has vanished so suddenly out of our sight.'

'I dare not do so,' replied Sancho, 'for on parting one step from you, fear seizes me and fills me with a thousand kinds of terror and affright. Let me say, once for all, that henceforth I do not stir a finger's-breadth from your presence.'

'Well,' replied Don Quixote, 'I am glad that thou dost build upon my valour, which shall not fail thee even though everything else fails thee. Follow me, then, and keep thine eyes open, so that we may find this strange man, who is no doubt the owner of the portmanteau.'

'Surely,' said Sancho, 'it were better not to find him, for if we should meet him, and he turned out to be the owner of the money, we should have to return it to him. Let us rather keep it faithfully until some one turns up to claim it, when perhaps I shall have spent it all, and in that case I shall be free from blame.'

'In that thou art mistaken, Sancho,' replied Don Quixote, 'for now that we have a suspicion who the owner is, we are bound to search him out and restore him his money.'

So saying Don Quixote led the way, and in a little time they came upon a dead mule, half devoured by dogs and crows; and as they were looking at it they heard a whistle, such as shepherds use, and there appeared at their left hand a great number of goats, and behind them on the top of the mountain was the Goatherd, who was quite an old man.

Don Quixote called to him, and begged him to come down to where they stood; and the Goatherd, after looking at them for a few minutes, in surprise at seeing them in this lonely spot, descended to where they stood.

'I wager,' he said, as he came towards them, 'that you are wondering how the mule came there that lies dead in that bottom. Well, it has been lying there these six months. Tell me, have you come across his master as yet?'

'We have fallen in with nobody,' replied Don Quixote, 'but a saddle cushion and a portmanteau, which we found not far from here.'

'I have also found the same portmanteau,' said the Goatherd, 'but I would never take it up nor approach it for fear some ill-luck should come upon me, or lest some one should accuse me of theft.'

'Tell me, my good fellow,' said Don Quixote, 'do you know who is the owner of these things?'

'All I can tell you is this,' said the Goatherd, 'that some six months ago, more or less, there arrived at one of our sheepfolds, some three leagues off, a young gentleman of comely presence mounted on that mule which lies dead there, and with the same saddle cushion and portmanteau that you have seen. He asked us which was the most hidden part of the mountain, and we told him that this was, which is certainly true, for if you go a league further on perhaps you might not find your way out, and indeed I marvel how you found your way in so readily. As soon as the young man had heard our answer he turned his bridle and went towards the place we showed him, and made towards these mountains. After that we did not see him for a good many days, until one day, when one of our shepherds came by with provisions, he attacked him and beat him, and carried off all the bread and cheese that he carried, and then fled away back again to the mountains. When we heard of this, some of us goatherds went to look for him, and spent al-

most two days in the most solitary places in the mountains, and in the end found him lurking in the hollow
part of a large cork-tree. He came out to us very meekly,
his clothes torn and his face burned by the sun, so that
we hardly knew him again. He saluted us courteously,
and in a few civil words told us not to wonder at his condition, for he was working out a penance placed upon
him for the sins he had committed. We begged him to
tell us who he was, but he would not do so. We begged
him also that when he had need of food he would tell us
where we might find him, and we would willingly bring
it to him, and told him there was no need to take it by
force. He thanked us very much for our offer, and asked
pardon for his violence, and promised in future to ask
food of our shepherds without giving annoyance to any
one. But even while he was speaking to us, he bit his lips
and bent his brows, and it was clear some fit of madness
was upon him, for he cried out: "O treacherous Fernando, here thou shalt pay me the injury thou didst me;
these hands shall rend thy heart!" and many other wild
and whirring words which he addressed to some Fernando. But at the same time he fell upon one of our
goatherds, and we had no little trouble to get him away.
Then without another word he fled to the briars and the
brambles, where we could not follow him. By this we
think that he has a madness which comes upon him at
times, for sometimes he will take his food from our shepherds with courtesy and humanity, at others he seizes it
by force, though they are ever willing to give it. We
have thought to take him by force to the town of Almo-

davar, to see if he can be cured, or to find out if he has any relatives to whom we can restore him. This, Sirs, is all that I can tell you of what you have asked me, and for certain he it is who is the owner of the things you have found.'

Don Quixote was greatly amazed by what he had heard, and determined to search him through the mountains, without leaving a corner or cave unsought until he had found him.

THE STORY
OF CARDENIO

CHAPTER XV

The Story of Cardenio

FORTUNE favoured Don Quixote in his search for the
strange owner of the portmanteau, for, even as he was
speaking to the Goatherd, he appeared at that very instant through a gorge of the mountain, murmuring to
himself words which one could not have understood near
at hand, much less afar off. His clothes were such as
have been described, only differing in this, that when he
drew near, Don Quixote noticed that he wore a leather
jerkin, which, though tattered and torn, was perfumed
with amber. From this he guessed that the man who
wore such garments was a person of quality. On coming
towards them, the youth addressed them in a hoarse tone

but with great courtesy, and Don Quixote returned his greetings with equal kindness, and, alighting from Rozinante, went to meet him, and clasping him in his arms, embraced him as though he had known him for a very long time.

Then the stranger, whom we may call the Tattered One, addressed the Knight of the Rueful Countenance in the following words: 'Truly, good Sir, whoever you may be, for I know you not, I thank you with all my heart for your grace and courtesy towards me, and wish only that I could repay you some of the kindness you shower on me.'

'So great is my desire to serve you,' replied Don Quixote, 'that I was fully resolved never to part out of these mountains until I had found you, and heard from your own lips whether there was any remedy for your grief. For it is a consolation in sorrow to have some one to condole with you. And I entreat you, Sir, tell me who you are, and what has brought you to live and die in these solitudes like a brute beast. For I swear by the high honour of Knighthood which I have received, that if you will tell me everything, I will either help you in all good earnest to overcome your troubles, or, if that cannot be, then I will assist in lamenting them.'

The Tattered One looked at Don Quixote from head to foot, and stared at him in amazement for a long time. At length he said: 'If you have anything to eat, give it to me, and after I have eaten I will do all that you ask in return for the kindness you show me.'

Sancho and the Goatherd then gave him what food

they had, and this he devoured with the eagerness of a wild beast, so that he seemed to swallow the food rather than chew it, and whilst he ate the others left him in peace. Having ended his dinner, he made signs to them to follow him, which they did, and he took them to a little meadow hard by that place at the back of the mountain.

Arriving there he laid himself down on the grass, the others doing the same, and he began as follows:—

'If it is your pleasure, Sirs, to hear of my misfortunes, you must promise me that you will not interrupt the thread of my sad story by questions or anything else, for directly you do I shall stop telling it.'

Don Quixote promised in the name of them all, and the Tattered One commenced his story.

'My name is Cardenio; the place of my birth one of the best cities in Andalusia; my lineage noble, my parents rich, and my misfortunes so great that I think no one was ever to be pitied as I am. There dwelt in the same city wherein I was born a damsel as noble and rich as I was, whose name was Lucinda. I loved, honoured, and adored Lucinda from earliest childhood, and she loved me with all the earnestness of youth. Our parents knew of our love, and were not sorry to see it, and so we grew up in mutual esteem and affection. Ah! how many letters have I written, and how many verses have I penned, and how many songs has she inspired! At length the time came when I could wait no longer, and I went to ask her of her father for my lawful wife. He answered that he thanked me for the desire I showed to honour him and to honour myself with his loved treasure, but that my father being alive, it was by strict right his business to make that demand. For if it were not done with his good will and pleasure, Lucinda was not the woman to be taken or given by stealth. I thanked him for his kindness, and, feeling there was reason in what he said, I hurried to my father to tell him my desires. At the moment I entered his room he was standing with a letter open in his hand, and before I could speak to him he gave it to me, saying as he did so: "By that letter, Cardenio, you may learn the desire that the Duke Ricardo has to do you favour." This Duke Ricardo, you must know, gentlemen, is a Grandee of Spain, whose dukedom is situated in the best part of all Andalusia. I took the letter and read it, and it was so very kind that it seemed to me wrong that my father should not do what he asked. For he wanted me as a companion—not as a servant—to his eldest son, and offered to advance me in life if he should find me worthy. I read the letter, and could see that it was no time now to speak to my father, who said to me: "Cardenio, thou must be ready in two days to depart, and to do all that the Duke desires, and be thankful that such a future lies open before thee."

'The time for my departure arrived. I spoke to my dear Lucinda and also to her afther, and begged him to wait for a while until I knew what the Duke Ricardo wanted of me, and until my future was certain. He promised not to bestow his daughter elsewhere, and she vowed to be always faithful to me, and so I left.

'I was indeed well received by the Duke Ricardo and

nobly treated. His elder son liked me well, and was kind
to me, but the one who rejoiced most at my coming was
Fernando, his second son, a young man who was both
noble, gallant, and very comely. In a short time he had
so made me his friend that there were no secrets between
us, and he told me all his thoughts and desires, and con-
fided to me a love affair of his own which caused him
much anxiety.

'He had fallen in love with the daughter of a farmer,
his father's vassal, whose parents were rich, and she herself was beautiful, modest, and virtuous. But he did not
dare to tell his father of his love because of their difference in rank, and though he had promised to marry this
farmer's daughter, he had come to fear that the Duke
would never consent to let him carry out his desire. He
told me that he could find no better mode of keeping
the remembrance of her beauty out of his mind than by
leaving home for some months; and he suggested that
we should both depart for awhile to my father's house,
under the pretence of going to buy horses, for the city
where I was born was a place where they bred the best
horses in the world.

'When I heard of his wishes I did all I could to
strengthen them, and urged him to carry out his plan,
which offered me a chance of seeing once more my dear
Lucinda.

'At last the Duke gave him leave, and ordered me to
go with him. We arrived at my native city, and my
father gave him the reception due to his rank. I again
saw Lucinda. My love for her increased, though indeed

it had never grown cold, and to my sorrow I told Don
Fernando all about it, for I thought by the laws of friendship it was not right to hide anything from him. I described her beauty, her grace, and her wit, with such
eloquence, that my praises stirred in him a desire to see
a damsel enriched by such rare virtues. To my misfortune I yielded to his wish, and took him with me one
night to a window where Lucinda and I were wont to
speak together. He stood mute, as one beside himself,
and from that moment he could speak nothing but
praises of my Lucinda. Yet I confess that I took no
pleasure in hearing her thus praised, because it roused
in me a strange feeling of jealousy. I did not fear the
faith and honour of Lucinda, but at the same time I felt
a hidden terror of the future. Now Don Fernando continued, as my friend, to read all the letters I sent to Lucinda, or she to me, under the pretence that he took great
delight in the wit of both of us, and it fell out that Lucinda asked me to send her a book of the Knightly Adventures of Amadis of Gaul.'

No sooner did Don Quixote hear the name of one of
his favourite heroes than he interrupted the story, saying:
'If, my good Sir, you had told me that your Lady Lucinda was a reader of knightly adventures, you need not
have said anything else to make me acknowledge her
wit. Waste no further words on her beauty and worth,
for now I assert that from her devotion to books of
Knighthood, the Lady Lucinda is the fairest and most
accomplished woman in all the world. Pardon my interruption, but when I hear anything said of the books of

Knights Errant, I can no more keep from speaking of them than the sunbeams can help giving forth warmth. Therefore forgive me, and proceed.'

While Don Quixote was speaking, Cardenio held his head down, his face grew sullen, and he bit his lip. When he looked up, he seemed to have forgotten all about his story, and in a burst of rage said: 'A plague on all your books of Knighthood! Amadis was a fool, and the Queen Madasima was a wicked woman.'

'By all that is good,' replied Don Quixote, in great anger—for this Queen was a favourite heroine of his—'it is a villainy to say such a thing. The Queen Madasima was a very noble lady, and whoever says or thinks the contrary lies like an errant coward, and this I will make him know a-horseback or a-foot, armed or disarmed, by night or day, as he liketh best.'

Cardenio stood gazing at Don Quixote strangely—for now the mad fit was on him—and hearing himself called liar and coward, he caught up a stone that was near him, and gave the Knight such a blow with it that he threw him backwards on the ground. Sancho Panza, seeing his Master so roughly handled, set upon the madman with his fists, but the Tattered One overthrew him with one blow and trampled him under his feet like dough. After this he departed into the wood very quietly.

Sancho got up and wanted to take vengeance on the Goatherd, who, he said, should have warned them about the madman. The Goatherd declared he had done so, and Sancho retorted that he had not; and from words they got to blows, and had seized each other by the beards, when Don Quixote parted them, saying that the Goatherd was in no way to blame for what had happened. He then again inquired where Cardenio was likely to be found, and the Goatherd repeated what he had said at first, that his abode was uncertain, but that if they went much about in those parts they would be sure to meet with him either mad or sane.

CHAPTER XVI

Of the Strange Adventures that happened to the
Knight of the Mancha in the Brown Mountains,
and of the Penance he did there in
imitation of Beltenebros

DON QUIXOTE took leave of the Goatherd, and, mounting
once again on Rozinante, he commanded Sancho to follow him, who obeyed, but with a very ill will. They travelled slowly, entering the thickest and roughest part of the
mountains, and at last Sancho Panza, who was growing
very impatient, burst out: 'Good Sir Don Quixote, let me
speak what is on my mind, for it is a hard thing to go
about looking for adventures all one's life, and find nothing but trampelings under the feet, and tossings in blan-
kets, and stoning, and blows, and buffets.'

'Speak on,' replied his Master, 'for I will hear what
thou hast to say.'

'Then,' replied Sancho, 'I would know what benefit
your Worship could reap by taking the part of the Queen
Magimasas, or whatever you call her. For if you had let
it pass, I believe the madman would have finished his
tale, and I should have escaped a beating.'

'In faith, Sancho,' replied Don Quixote, 'if thou knew-

ON QUIXOTE
DOING PENANCE

est as well as I do, how honourable a lady was Queen Madasima, thou wouldst rather say I behaved with great patience. Cardenio knew not what he was saying to call her wicked, and must have been out of his senses.'

'So say I,' said Sancho, 'and you ought not to take notice of the words of a madman.'

'Against sane and mad,' replied Don Quixote, 'is every Knight Errant bound to stand up for the honour of women, whoever they may be. Be silent, therefore, and meddle not with what does not concern thee. Understand that all I do is guided by the rules of Knighthood, which are better known to me than to any Knight that ever lived.'

'Sir!' replied Sancho, 'is there any rule of Knighthood which obliges us to wander among the mountains looking for a madman, who, if he is found, will probably break our heads again?'

'Peace, I say, Sancho, once again!' exclaimed Don Quixote, 'for thou must know that it is not only the desire of finding the madman that brings me into these wilds, but because I have in mind to carry out an adventure that shall bring me eternal fame and renown over the whole face of the earth.'

'Is it a dangerous adventure?' asked Sancho.

'That is according as it turns out,' replied Don Quixote. 'But I will keep you no longer in the dark about it. You must know that Amadis of Gaul was the most perfect of all the Knights Errant. And as he was the morning star and the sun of all valiant Knights, so am I wise in imitating all he did. And I remember that when his

Lady Oriana disdained his love, he showed his wisdom, virtue, and manhood by changing his name to Beltenebros and retiring to a wild country, there to perform a penance. And as I may more easily imitate him in this than in slaying giants, beheading serpents, killing monsters, destroying armies, and putting navies to flight, and because this mountain seems to fit for the purpose, I intend myself to do penance here.'

'But what is it that your Worship intends to do in this out of the way spot?" asked Sancho.

'Have not I told thee already,' replied his Master, 'that I mean to copy Amadis of Gaul, by acting here the part of a despairing, mad, and furious lover?'

'I believe,' continued Sancho, 'that the Knights who went through these penances must have had some reason for so doing, but what cause has your Worship for going mad? What Lady hath disdained you? How has the Lady Dulcinea of Toboso ever treated you unkindly?'

'That is just the point of it,' said Don Quixote; 'for a Knight Errant to go mad for good reason has no merit in it, but the whole kernel of the matter is to go mad without a cause. Therefore, Sancho, waste no more time, for mad I am, and mad I shall remain, until thou return again with the answer to a letter which I mean to send with thee to my Lady Dulcinea. If the answer is such as I deserve, my penance will end, but if on the contrary I shall run mad in good earnest. But tell me, Sancho, hast thou kept safely the helmet of Mambrino?'

'Really, Sir Knight,' answered Sancho, 'I cannot listen patiently to some things your Worship says, and I sometimes think all you tell me of Knighthood is nothing but a pack of lies. For to hear your Worship say that a barber's basin is Mambrino's helmet, and not to find out your mistake in four days, makes one wonder whether one is standing on one's head or one's heels. I carry the basin right enough in my baggage, all battered and dented, and intend to take it home and put it to rights, and soap my beard in it when I return to my wife and children.'

'Ah, Sancho,' replied Don Quixote, 'I think that thou hast the shallowest pate that ever any Squire had or hath in this world. Is it possible thou hast so long travelled with me and not found out that all the adventures of Knights Errant appear illusions, follies, and dreams, and turn out all contrariwise? So this that thou callest a barber's basin is to me Mambrino's helmet, and to another person has some other shape altogether. Not that it has all these shapes, but these things are the work of wicked enchanters or magicians, who transform everything, making things seem what they please in order to annoy us.'

By this time they had arrived at the foot of a lofty mountain, which stood like a huge rock apart from all the rest. Close by glided a smooth river, hemmed in on every side by a green and fertile meadow. Around were many fine trees and plants and flowers, which made the spot a most delightful one.

'Here!' cried Don Quixote in a loud voice, 'I elect to do my penance. Here shall the tears from my eyes swell and limpid streams, and here shall the sighs of my heart

stir the leaves of every mountain tree. O Dulcinea of
Toboso, day of my night and star of my fortunes, consider the pass to which I am come, and return a favour-
able answer to my wishes!'

With this he alighted from Rozinante, and, taking off
his saddle and bridle, gave him a slap on his haunches,
and said: 'He gives thee liberty that wants it himself, O
steed, famous for thy swiftness and the great works thou
hast done!'

When Sancho heard all this he could not help saying:
'I wish Dapple were here, for he deserves at least as long
a speech in his praise; but truly, Sir Knight, if my journey
with your letter, and your penance here, are really to
take place, it would be better to saddle Rozinante again,
that he may supply the want of mine Ass.'

'As thou likest about that,' said Don Quixote; 'but thou
must not depart for three days as yet, during which time
thou shalt see what I will say and do for my Lady's sake,
that thou mayest tell her all about it.'

'But what more can I see,' asked Sancho, 'than what I
have already seen?'

'Thou are well up in the matter, certainly,' replied his
Master, 'for as yet I have done nothing, and if I am to be
a despairing lover, I must tear my clothes, and throw
away mine armour, and beat my head against these
rocks, with many other things that shall make thee
marvel.'

'For goodness' sake,' cried Sancho, 'take care how you
go knocking your head against rocks, for you might happen to come up against so ungracious a rock that it would

put an end to the penance altogether. If the knocks on the head are necessary, I should content yourself, seeing that this madness is all make-believe, with striking your head on some softer thing, and leave the rest to me, for I will tell your Lady that I saw you strike your head on the point of a rock that was harder than a diamond.'

'I thank thee, Sancho, for thy good will,' replied the Knight, 'but the rules of Knighthood forbid me to act or to speak a lie, and therefore the knocks of the head must be real solid knocks, and it will be necessary for thee to leave me some lint to cure them, seeing that fortune has deprived us of that precious Balsam.'

'It was worse to lose the Ass,' said Sancho, 'seeing that with him we lost lint and everything; but pray, your Worship, never mention that horrible Balsam again, for the very name of it nearly turns me inside out. And now write your letter, and let me saddle Rozinante and be-gone, for I warrant when I once get to Toboso I will tell the Lady Dulcinea such strange things of your follies and madness, that I shall make her as soft as a glove even though I find her harder than a cork-tree. And with her sweet and honied answer I will return as speedily as a witch on a broomstick, and release you from your pen-ance.'

'But how shall we write a letter here?' said Don Quix-ote.

'And how can you write the order for the handing over to me of the ass-colts?' asked Sancho.

'Seeing there is no paper,' said the Knight, 'we might, like the ancients, write on waxen tablets, but that wax is as hard to find as paper. But now that I come to think of it, there is Cardenio's pocket-book. I will write on that, and thou shalt have the matter of it written out in a good round hand at the first village wherein thou shalt find a schoolmaster.'

'But what is to be done about the signature?' asked Sancho.

'The letters of Amadis were never signed,' replied Don Quixote.

'That is all very well,' said Sancho, 'but the paper for the three asses must be signed, for if it be copied out they shall say it is false, and then I shall not get the ass-colts.'

'Well, then, the order for the ass-colts shall be signed in the book,' said Don Quixote; 'and as for the love-letter, thou shalt put this ending to it, "Yours till death, the Knight of the Rueful Countenance." And it will be no great matter that it goes in a strange hand, for as well as I remember Dulcinea can neither read nor write, nor has she ever seen my handwriting. For indeed, during the twelve years I have been loving her more dearly than the light of my eyes, I have only seen her four times, and I doubt if she hath ever noticed me at all, so closely have her father Lorenzo Corchuelo, and her mother Aldonza brought her up.'

'Ha! ha!' cried Sancho, 'then the Lady Dulcinea of Toboso is the daughter of Lorenzo Corchuelo, and is called Aldonza Corchuelo?'

'That is she,' said Don Quixote, 'and a lady worthy to be the Empress of this wide universe.'

'I know her very well,' replied Sancho, 'and can tell you that she can throw an iron bar with the strongest lad in our village. She is a girl of mettle, tall and stout, and a sturdy lass that can hold her own with any Knight Errant in the world. Out upon her, what an arm she hath! Why, I saw her one day stand on top of the church belfry, to call her father's servants from the fields, and, though they were half a league off, they heard her as though she were in the next field; and the best of her is there is nothing coy about her, but she jokes with all and makes game and jest of everybody. To be frank with you, Sir Don Quixote, I have been living under a great mistake, for, really and truly, I thought all this while that the Lady Dulcinea was some great Princess with whom your Worship was in love.'

'I have told thee, Sancho, many times before now,' said Don Quixote, 'that thou art a very great babbler. Understand, then, that my Lady Dulcinea is to me as good and beautiful as any Princess in the world, and that is enough.'

With these words he took out the pocket-book, and, going aside, began to write with great gravity. When he had ended, he called Sancho to him and read him the following letter:

SOVEREIGN LADY,

The sore wounded one, O sweetest Dulcinea of Toboso, sends thee the health which he wants himself. If thy beauty disdain me, I cannot live. My good Squire Sancho will give thee ample account, O ungrateful fair one, of the penance I do for love of thee. Should it be thy pleasure to favour me, I am thine. If not, by ending my life I shall satisfy both thy cruelty and my desires.

Thine until death,

THE KNIGHT OF THE RUEFUL COUNTENANCE.

'By my father's life,' said Sancho, 'it is the noblest thing that ever I heard in my life; and now will your Worship write the order for the three ass-colts?'

'With pleasure,' answered Don Quixote, and he did as he was desired.

'And now,' said Sancho, 'let me saddle Rozinante and be off. For I intend to start without waiting to see those mad pranks your Worship is going to play. There is one thing I am afraid of, though, and that is, that on my return I shall not be able to find the place where I leave you, it is so wild and difficult.'

'Take the marks well, and when thou shouldst return I will mount to the tops of the highest rocks. Also it will be well to cut down some boughs and strew them after you as you go, that they may serve as marks to find your way back, like the clue in Theseus' labyrinth.'

Sancho did this, and, not heeding his Master's request to stay and see him go through some mad tricks in order that he might describe them to Dulcinea, he mounted Rozinante and rode away.

He had not got more than a hundred paces when he returned and said: 'Sir, what you said was true, and it would be better for my conscience if I saw the follies you are about to do before I describe them to your Lady.'

'Did I not tell thee so?' said Don Quixote; 'wait but a minute.'

Then stripping himself in all haste of most of his clothes, Don Quixote began cutting capers and turning somersaults in his shirt tails, until even Sancho was satisfied that he might truthfully tell the Lady Dulcinea that her lover was mad, and so, turning away, he started in good earnest upon his journey.

THE CURATE
& THE BARBER
IN DISGUISE

CHAPTER XVII

Of Sancho's Journey to the Lady Dulcinea

DON QUIXOTE, left to himself, climbed to the top of a high mountain, and spent his days making poems about the beautiful Dulcinea, which he recited to the rocks and trees around him. In this, and in calling upon the nymphs of the streams, and the satyrs of the woods, to hear his cries, did he pass his time while Sancho was away.

As for his Squire, turning out on the highway, he took the road which led to Toboso, and arrived the next day at the Inn where he had been tossed in a blanket. He no sooner saw it than he imagined that he was once again flying through the air, and he half made up his mind that he would not enter the Inn, although it was now dinner-hour and he felt a marvellous longing to taste some cooked meat again, as he had eaten nothing but cold fare for a good many days.

This longing made him draw near to the Inn, remaining still in some doubt as to whether he should enter it or not.

As he stood musing, there came out of the Inn two persons who recognised him at once, and the one said to the other: 'Tell me, Sir Curate, is not that horseman riding there Sancho Panza, who departed with Don Quixote to be his Squire?'

'It is,' said the Curate, 'and that is Don Quixote's horse.'

They knew him well enough, for they were Don Quixote's friends, the Curate and the Barber, who not so long ago had helped to burn his books and wall up his library; so, wanting to learn news of Don Quixote, they went up to him and said: 'Friend Sancho Panza, where have you left your Master?'

Sancho Panza knew them instantly, but wanted to conceal the place and manner in which the Knight remained, and answered that his Master was kept in a certain place by affairs of the greatest importance of which he must say nothing.

'That will not do, friend Sancho,' said the Barber. 'If thou dost not tell us where he is, we shall believe that thou hast robbed and slain him, seeing that thou art riding his horse. Verily thou must find us the owner of the steed, or it will be the worse for thee.'

'Your threats do not trouble me, for I am not one who

would rob or murder anybody, and, for my Master, he is enjoying himself doing penance in the Brown Mountains, where I have just left him.'

Then Sancho told them from beginning to end how his Master was carrying out his penance, and of the mad pranks he intended to perform, and how he, Sancho, was bearing a letter to the Lady Dulcinea of Toboso, who was none other than the daughter of Lorenzo Corchuelo, with whom the Knight was head and ears in love.

Both of them were amazed at what they heard, although they knew something of Don Quixote's madness already. They asked Sancho to show them the letter he was carrying to the Lady Dulcinea. Sancho told them it was written in the pocket-book, and that he was ordered to get it copied out at the first village he came to.

The Curate told him that if he would show it to them he would make a fair copy of it for him. Then Sancho thrust his hand into his bosom to search for the little book, but he could not find it, nor would he have found it if he had hunted until Doomsday, for he had left it with Don Quixote, who had quite forgotten to give it to him, nor had he remembered to ask for it when he came away. When Sancho discovered that the book was lost, his face grew as pale as death, and feeling all over his body he saw clearly that it was not to be found. Without more ado he laid hold of his beard, and with both his fists plucked out half his hair and gave himself half a dozen blows about his face and nose, so that he was soon bathed in his own blood.

Seeing this, the Curate and the Barber asked him what was the matter, that he should treat himself so ill.

'What is the matter?' cried poor Sancho. 'Why, I have let slip through my fingers three of the finest ass-colts you ever saw.'

'How so?' asked the Barber.

'Why, I have lost the pocket-book,' replied Sancho, 'which had in it not only the letter for Dulcinea, but also a note of hand signed by my Master addressed to his Niece, ordering her to give me three ass-colts of the four or five that were left at his house.' So saying, he told them the story of his lost Dapple.

The Curate comforted him by telling him that as soon as they had found his Master they would get him to write out the paper again in proper form. With this Sancho took courage, and said if that could be done all would be right, for he cared not much for the loss of Dulcinea's letter as he knew it by heart.

'Say it then, Sancho,' said the Barber, 'and we will write it out.'

Then Sancho stood still and began to scratch his head and try to call the letter to memory. He stood first on one leg and then on the other, and looked first to heaven and then to earth, while he gnawed off half his nails, and at the end of a long pause said: 'I doubt if I can remember all, but it began, "High and unsavoury Lady."'

'I warrant you,' interrupted the Barber, it was not "unsavoury" but "sovereign Lady."'

'So it was,' cried Sancho; 'and then there was something about the wounded one sending health and sickness and what not to the ungrateful fair, and so it scrambled along until it ended in "Yours till death, the Knight of the Rueful Countenance." '

They were both much amused at Sancho's good memory, and praised it highly, asking him to repeat the letter once or twice more to them, so that they might be able to write it down when they got a chance. Three times did Sancho repeat it, and each time he made as many new mistakes. Then he told them other things about his Master, but never a word about being tossed in a blanket, although he refused, without giving any reason, to enter the Inn, though he begged them to bring him something nice and hot to eat, and some barley for Rozinante, when they had finished their own repast.

With that they went into the Inn, and after a while the Curate brought him some meat, which Sancho was very glad to see.

Now whilst the Curate and the Barber were in the Inn they discussed together the best means of bringing Don Quixote back to his home, and the Curate hit upon a plan which fitted in well with Don Quixote's humour, and seemed likely to be successful. This plan was, as he told the Barber, to dress himself like a wandering damsel, while the Barber took the part of her Squire, and in this disguise they were to go to where Don Quixote was undergoing his penance, and the Curate, pretending that he was an afflicted and sorely distressed damsel, was to demand of him a boon, which as a valiant Knight Errant he could not refuse.

The service which the damsel was to ask was that Don

Quixote would follow her where she should lead him, to right a wrong which some wicked Knight had done her. Besides this, she was to pray him not to command her to unveil herself or inquire as to her condition, until he had done her right against the wicked Knight. And thus they hoped to lead Don Quixote back to his own village, and afterwards to cure him of his mad ideas.

The Curate's notion pleased the Barber well, and they resolved to carry it out. They borrowed of the Innkeeper's wife a gown and a head-dress, leaving with her in exchange the Curate's new cassock. The Barber made for himself a great beard of a red ox's tail in which the Innkeeper used to hang his horse-comb.

The Innkeeper's wife asked them what they wanted these things for, and the Curate told her shortly all about Don Quixote's madness, and how this disguise was necessary to bring him away from the mountains where he had taken up his abode.

The Innkeeper and his wife then remembered all about their strange guest, and told the Barber and the Curate all about him and his Balsam, and how Sancho had fared with the blanket. Then the Innkeeper's wife dressed up the Curate so cleverly that it could not have been better done. She attired him in a stuff gown with bands of black velvet several inches broad, and a bodice and sleeves of green velvet trimmed with white satin, both of which might have been made in the days of the Flood. The Curate would not consent to wear a head-dress like a woman's, but put on a white quilted linen nightcap, which he carried to sleep in. Then with two strips of black stuff he made himself a mask and fixed it on, and this covered his face and beard very neatly. He then put on his large hat, and, wrapping himself in his cloak, seated himself like a woman sideways on his mule, whilst the Barber mounted his, with a beard reaching down to his girdle, made, as was said, from a red ox's tail.

They now took their leave, and all at the Inn wished them a good success; but they had not gone very far when the Curate began to dread that he was not doing right in dressing up as a woman and gadding about in such a costume, even on so good an errand. He therefore proposed to the Barber that he should be the distressed damsel, and he, the Curate, would take the part of the Squire and teach him what to say and how to behave. Sancho now came up to them, and, seeing them in their strange dresses, could not contain his laughter.

The Curate soon threw off his disguise, and the Barber did the same, and both resolved not to dress up any more until they should come nearer to Don Quixote, when the Barber should be the distressed damsel and the Curate should be the Squire.

Then they pursued their journey towards the Brown Mountains, guided by Sancho, to whom they explained that is was necessary that his Master should be led away from his penance, if he was ever to become an Emperor and be in a position to give Sancho his desired Island.

THE STORY OF
CARDENIO·
· CONTINUED

CHAPTER XVIII

The Story of Cardenio continued

THE next day they arrived at the place where Sancho had left the boughs strewn along his path, and there he told them they were near to Don Quixote, and that they had better get dressed. For they had told Sancho part of their plan to take away his Master from this wretched penance he was performing, and warned him not to tell the Knight who they were. They also said that if Don Quixote asked, as they were sure he would, whether he had delivered his letter to Dulcinea, he was to say that he had done so; but as his Lady could not read, she had sent a message that he was to return to her. Sancho listened to all this talk, and said he would remember everything, for he was anxious that his Master should give up

penances and go forth again in search of Islands. He
also suggested that it were best he should go on in advance, as perhaps the message from Dulcinea would of
itself be enough to bring Don Quixote away from the
mountains.

With that, Sancho went off into the mountain gorges,
leaving the other two behind by a stream overhung with
pleasant trees and rocks.

It was one of the hottest days of August, when in those
parts the heat is very great, and it was about three in the
afternoon when Sancho left them. The two were resting
in the shade at their ease when they heard the sound of
a voice, not accompanied by any instrument, but singing
very sweetly and melodiously. The song surprised them
not a little, for this did not seem the place in which to
find so good a singer.

The singer finished his song, and the Barber and Curate, in wonder and delight, listened for more. But as
silence continued, they agreed to go in search of this
strange musician. As they were moving away he again
burst into song, and at the end of this, uttered a deep
sigh, and the music was changed into sobs and heart-
rending moans.

They had not gone far in their search when, in turning
the corner of a rock, they saw a man of the same figure
that Sancho had described to them when he had told
them the story of Cardenio. The Curate at once went
up to him, and in a kindly manner begged him to quit
this wretched, wandering life, lest he should perish
among the mountains.

Cardenio, who was in his right mind at this time, and quite free from his mad fit, replied: 'Whoever you may be, good Sirs, I see clearly that, unworthy as I am, there are yet human beings who would show me kindness by persuading me to live in some better place; and I know myself how this terrible madness masters me, and many blame my outrageous conduct rather than pity my misfortunes. But if you will listen to my story, you will know why I have been driven here, what has made me mad, and will understand how far I ought to be blamed, and how much I may be pitied.'

The Curate and the Barber, who wanted nothing better than to learn the cause of his woe from his own lips, asked him to tell his story, and promised they would do all they could for his consolation.

Upon this Cardenio began his story, and told them all that he had told Don Quixote, until he came to the book that Lucinda had borrowed about Amadis of Gaul. There was no interruption from Don Quixote on this occasion, so Cardenio went on to tell them how, when Lucinda returned the book he found in it a letter full of the most tender wishes beautifully expressed.

'It was this letter,' continued Cardenio, 'that moved me to again ask Lucinda for wife; it was this letter also which made Don Fernando determine to ruin me before my happiness could be complete. I told Don Fernando how matters stood with me, and how her father expected mine to ask for Lucinda, and how I dared not speak to my father about it for fear he should refuse his consent; not because he was ignorant of the beauty and worth of

Lucinda, but because he did not wish me to marry so soon, or at least not until he had seen what the Duke Ricardo would do for me. I told Don Fernando that I could not venture to speak to my father about it, and he offered to speak on my behalf, and persuade my father to ask for Lucinda's hand.

'How could I imagine that with a gentleman like Fernando, my own friend, such a thing as treachery was possible? But so it was! And my friend, as I thought him, knowing that my presence was a stumbling-block to his plans, asked me to go to his elder brother's to borrow some money from him to pay for six horses which Fernando had bought in the city. It never entered my thoughts to imagine his villainy, and I went with a right good will to do his errand. That night I spoke with Lucinda, and told her what had been arranged between me and Fernando, telling her to hope that all would turn out well. As I left her, tears filled her eyes, and we both seemed full of misery and alarm, tokens, as I now think, of the dark fate that awaited me. I reached the town to which I was sent, and delivered my letters to Don Fernando's brother. I was well received, but there seemed no haste to send me back again, and I was put off with many excuses about the difficulty of raising the money that Don Fernando needed. In this way I rested several days, much to my disgust, and it seemed to me impossible to live apart from Lucinda for so long a time.

'But on the fourth day after I had arrived, there came a man in search of me with a letter, which, by the handwriting, I knew to be Lucinda's. I opened it, not without fear, knowing that it must be some serious matter which would lead her to write to me, seeing she did it so rarely. I asked the bearer, before I read the letter, who had given it to him, and how long it had been on the way. He answered that, passing by chance at midday through a street in my native city, a very beautiful lady had called to him from a window. "Poor thing," said he, "her eyes were all bedewed with tears, and she spoke hurriedly, saying: 'Brother, if thou art a good man, as thou seemest to be, I pray thee take this letter to the person named in the address, and in so doing thou shalt do me a great service. And that thou mayest not want money to do it, take what thou shalt find wrapped in that handkerchief.'

' "So saying she threw out of the window a handkerchief in which was wrapped a hundred *reals*, this ring of gold which I carry here, and this letter which I have given you. I made signs to her that I would do what she bade, and as I knew you very well I made up my mind not to trust any other messenger, but to come myself, and so I have travelled this journey, which you know is some eighteen leagues, in but sixteen hours."

'Whilst the kind messenger was telling his story, I remained trembling with the letter in my hand, until at last I took courage and opened it, when these words caught my eyes:—

' "The promise Don Fernando made to you to persuade your father to speak to mine, he has kept after his own fashion. Know, then, that he has himself asked me for wife, and my father, carried away by his rank and position, has agreed to his wishes, so that in two days we are to be privately married. Imagine how I feel, and consider if you should not come at once. Let me hope that this reaches your hand ere mine be joined to his who keeps his promised faith so ill."

'Such were the words of her letter, and they caused me at once to set out on my journey without waiting for the despatch of Don Fernando's business, for now I knew that it was not a matter of buying horses, but the pursuit of his own wretched pleasure, that had led to my being sent to his brother. The rage which I felt for Don Fernando, joined to the fear I had of losing the jewel I had won by so many years of patient love, seemed to lend me wings, and I arrived at my native city as swiftly as though I had flown, just in time to see and speak with Lucinda. I entered the city secretly, and left my mule at the house of the honest man who had brought my letter, and went straight to the little iron gate where I had so often met Lucinda.

'There I found her, and as soon as she saw me she said in deep distress: "Cardenio, I am attired in wedding garments, and in the hall there waits for me the traitor, Don Fernando, and my covetous father, with other witnesses, who shall see my death rather than my wedding. Be not troubled, dear friend, for if I cannot persuade them to give me my freedom, I can at least end my life with this dagger."

'I answered her in great distress, saying: "Sweet lady, if thou carriest a dagger, I also carry a sword to defend thy life, or to kill myself, should fortune be against us."

'I believe she did not hear all I said, for she was hastily called away, and I aroused myself from my grief, as best I could, and went into the house, for I knew well all the entrances and exits. Then, without being seen, I managed to place myself in a hollow formed by the window of the great hall, which was covered by two pieces of tapestry drawn together, whence I could see all that went on in the hall without any one seeing me.

'The bridegroom entered the hall, wearing his ordinary dress. His groomsman was a first cousin of Lucinda's, and no one else was in the room but the servants of the house. In a little while Lucinda came out of her dressing-room with her mother and two of her maids. My anxiety gave me no time to note what she wore. I was only able to mark the colours, which were crimson and white; and I remember the glimmer with which the jewels and precious stones shone in her head-dress. But all this was as nothing to the singular beauty of her fair golden hair.

'When they were all stood in the hall, the Priest of the parish entered, and, taking each by the hand, asked: "Will you, Lady Lucinda, take the Lord Don Fernando for your lawful husband?" I thrust my head and neck out of the tapestry to hear what Lucinda answered. The Priest stood waiting for a long time before she gave it, and then, when I expected, nay, almost hoped, that she would take out the dagger to stab herself, or unloose her tongue to speak the truth, or make some confession of her love for me, I heard her say in a faint and languishing voice, "I will."

'Then Don Fernando said the same, and giving her the ring, the knot was tied. But when the Bridegroom approached to embrace her, she put her hand to her heart and fell fainting in her mother's arms.

'It remains only for me to tell in what a state I was, when in that "Yes!" I saw all my hopes at an end. I burned with rage and jealousy. All the house was in a tumult when Lucinda fainted, and, her mother unclasping her dress to give her air, found in her bosom a paper, which Fernando seized and went aside to read by the light of a torch. Whilst he read it he fell into a chair and covered his face with his hands in melancholy discontent.

'Seeing every one was in confusion I ventured forth, not caring where I went, not having even a desire to take vengeance on my enemies. I left the house, and came to where I had left my mule, which I caused to be saddled. Then without a word of farewell to any one I rode out of the city, and never turned my head to look back at it again.

"All night I travelled, and about dawn I came to one of the entrances to these mountains, through which I wandered three days at random. I then left my mule, and such things as I had, and took to living in these wilds. My most ordinary dwelling is in the hollow of a cork-tree, which is large enough to shelter this wretched body. The goatherds who live among these mountains give me food out of charity. They tell me, when they meet me in my wits, that at other times I rush out at them and seize with violence the food they would offer me in kindness.

'I know that I do a thousand mad things, but without Lucinda I shall never recover my reason, and I feel certain that my misery can only be ended by death.'

THE DISCOVERY
OF DOROTHEA

CHAPTER XIX

The Story of Dorothea, who loved Don
Fernando

As soon as Cardenio had finished his melancholy story,
the Curate was about to offer him some consolation,
when he was stopped by hearing a mournful voice calling out: 'Oh that I could find an end to this life of misery!
Alas, how much more agreeable to me is the company of
these rocks and thickets than the society of faithless man!
Would that I had any one to advise me in difficulty, to
comfort me in distress, or to avenge my wrongs!'

This was overheard by the Curate and all who were
with him, and thinking that the person who spoke must
be hard by, they went to search, and had not gone

152

twenty paces when they saw behind a large rock a boy sitting under an ash-tree. He wore a peasant's dress, but as he was bending down to wash his feet in the brook, his head was turned from them. They approached softly and without speaking, while his whole attention was employed in bathing his legs in the stream. They wondered at the whiteness and beauty of his feet, that did not seem formed to tread the furrows, or follow the cattle or the plough, as his dress seemed to suggest. The Curate, who was ahead of the rest, made signs to them to crouch down, or hide themselves behind a rock. This done, they all gazed at the beautiful youth, who was clad in a grey jacket, and wore breeches and hose of the same cloth, with a grey hunting-cap on his head. Having washed his delicate feet, he wiped them with a handkerchief which he took out of his cap, and in doing so he raised his head, showing to those who were looking at him a face of such exquisite beauty that Cardenio murmured: 'Since this is not Lucinda, it can be no earthly but some celestial being.'

The youth took off his cap, and, shaking his head, a wealth of hair, that Apollo might have envied, fell down upon his shoulders, and discovered to them all that the peasant was not only a woman, but one of the most delicate and handsome women they had ever seen. Even Cardenio had to admit to himself that only Lucinda could rival her in beauty. Her golden locks fell down in such length and quantity that they not only covered her shoulders, but concealed everything except her feet, and the bystanders more than ever desired to know who this

mysterious beauty might be. Some one advanced, and at
the noise the beauteous phantasy raised her head, and
thrust aside her locks with both hands, to see what it was
that had startled her. No sooner did she perceive them
then she started up, and, without staying to put on her
shoes or tie up her hair, seized her bundle, and took to
flight full of alarm, but she had not run six yards when
her delicate feet, unable to bear the roughness of the
stones, failed her, and she fell to the ground.

They all ran to her assistance, and the Curate, who was
first, said: 'Stay, Madam, whosoever you are; those you
see here have no desire to harm you, and there is therefore no necessity whatever for flight.'

To this she made no reply, being ashamed and confused, but the Curate, taking her hand, continued in a
kindly manner: 'Madam, it can be no slight cause that
has hidden your beauty in such an unworthy disguise,
and brought you to this lonely place where we have
found you. Let us at least offer you our advice and counsel in your distress, for no sorrow can be so great that
kind words may not be of service. Therefore, Madam,
tell us something of your good or evil fortune, that we
may help you in your troubles as best we can.'

At first, while the Curate spoke, the disguised damsel
stood rapt in attention, and gaped and gazed at them all
as if she were some stupid villager, who did not understand what was said; but finding that the Curate understood something of her secret, she sighed deeply, and
said: 'Since these mountains canont conceal me, and my
poor hair betrays my secret, it would be vain for me to

pretend things which you could not be expected to believe. Therefore I thank you all, gentlemen, for your kindness and courtesy, and I will tell you something of my misfortunes, not to win your pity, but that you may know why it is I wander here alone and in this strange disguise.'

All this was said in such a sweet voice, and in so sensible a manner, that they again assured her of their wish to serve her, and begged that she would tell them her story.

To this she replied by putting on her shoes and binding up her hair, and seating herself upon a rock in the midst of her three hearers. Then, brushing away a few tears from her eyes, she began in a clear voice the story of her life.

'In the Province of Andalusia there is a certain town from which a great Duke takes his name, which makes him one of our Grandees, as they are called in Spain. He has two sons. The elder is heir to his estates, the younger is heir to I know not what, unless it be his father's evil qualities. To this nobleman my parents are vassals, of humble and low degree, but still so rich that if nature had gifted them with birth equal to their wealth, I should have been nobly born, nor should I now have suffered these strange misfortunes. They are but farmers and plain people, and what they mostly prized was their daughter, whom they thought to be the best treasure they had. As they had no other child, they were almost too affectionate and indulgent, and I was their spoilt child. And as I was the mistress of their affection, so also was I mistress of all their goods. I kept the reckoning of their oil-mills, their wine-presses, their cattle and sheep, their beehives—in a word, of all that a rich farmer like my father could possess. I engaged and dismissed the servants, and was the stewardess of the estate. The spare hours that were left from the management of the farm I spent with the needle, the lace cushion, and the distaff, or else I would read some good book or practise upon my harp.

'This was the life that I led in my father's house. And though I seldom went abroad except to church, yet it seems I had attracted the eyes of the Duke's younger son, Don Fernando, for so he was called.'

No sooner did she mention the name of Don Fernando than Cardenio's face changed colour, and the Curate and Barber noticing it, feared that he would burst out into one of his mad fits. But he did nothing but tremble and remain silent, and the girl continued her story.

'No sooner, then, had Don Fernando seen me than he was smitten with love for me, and from that moment I had no peace. I could not sleep for his serenades. I had numerous letters from him, full of declarations of love, and at last at his earnest entreaty we had many meetings. But though he talked much of love, yet I knew that his father would not allow him to marry the daughter of one of his own vassals, and my parents both assured me that the Duke would never consent to our marriage.

'One evening Don Fernando gave me a beautiful ring, and promised that he would always be true to me, and from that moment I felt that I was betrothed to him, and that he really intended, in spite of the Duke's opposition, to make me his wife. For some days I lived in the greatest joy, and Don Fernando came constantly to see me, but after a while his visits grew less frequent, and at last ceased altogether, and I heard that he had gone on a visit to another city.

'I waited in hopes of receiving a letter from him, but none came. Ah, how sad and bitter those days and hours were to me, when I first began to doubt and even to disbelieve in my lover's faith! I had to keep watch on my tears, and wear a happy face for fear my parents should find out the reason of my unhappiness. All this time of doubt, however, came to end at an instant. For at last it was announced in the town that Don Fernando had married, in the city where he was visiting, a damsel of exceeding beauty and of very noble birth called Lucinda, and there were many strange tales told of their wedding.'

Cardenio, hearing the name of Lucinda, did nothing but shrug his shoulders, bow his head, and shed bitter tears. But yet, for all that, Dorothea, for such was the maiden's name, did not interrupt the thread of her story, but continued.

'When this doleful news reached my ears, I was inflamed with rage and fury. I ordered one of my father's shepherds to attend me, and without saying a word to my parents, I packed up some dresses and some money and jewels, and set off on foot for the city where Don Fernando had gone, that I might get from him at least some explanation of his wickedness. In two days and a half I arrived at my journey's end, and the first person I asked told me the whole story of Don Fernando's wedding. He told me that at the time of the wedding, after Lucinda had uttered her consent to be Fernando's wife, she had fainted, and there fell from her bosom a letter written in her own hand, in which she said that she could not be the wife of Don Fernando, because she was betrothed to Cardenio, a gentleman of that city. The letter went on to say that she intended to kill herself at the end of the ceremony, and upon her was found a dagger, which seemed to bear out what she said. Don Fernando seeing this, and thinking that Lucinda had mocked him, would have stabbed her with the dagger had her parents not prevented him. After this, I was told, Don Fernando fled, and I learned that this Cardenio had been present at the wedding, and, hearing her words, had vanished from the city in despair, leaving a letter behind, declaring the wrongs Lucinda had done to him. The whole city were talking of these terrible things, and they talked the more when it was known that Lucinda was missing from her father's house, and that her parents had almost lost their reason in their distress. When I heard all these things I made up my mind I would find Don Fernando, married or unmarried. But before I left the city on my search, I was told there was a proclamation made by the public crier, offering a large reward for any one who should bring me back to my parents. Fearing that this might tempt the shepherd to betray my whereabouts, I made my escape from the city, and in this disguise came to the Brown Mountains, where I have lived for some months with an old Goatherd, and I help him to tend his goats. Here I have managed to pass as a peasant lad until my hair betrayed me to you gentlemen as what I am, a distressed and unfortunate maiden. This is indeed the true story of my tragedy, for which consolation is in vain, and relief, I fear me, impossible.'

CHAPTER XX

Of the pleasant Plan they carried out to persuade
Don Quixote not to continue his Penance

WHEN the unfortunate Dorothea had finished her story, she remained silent, her face flushed with sorrow; and as the Priest was about to comfort her, Cardenio took her by the hand and said: 'Lady, thou art the beautiful Dorothea, daughter unto rich Cleonardo.'

Dorothea was amazed when she heard her father's name spoken by a person of such wretched appearance as Cardenio, and answered: 'Who art thou, friend, that knowest so well my father's name? For, unless I am mistaken, I did not once name him throughout all my story.'

'I am,' said Cardenio, 'the unlucky one to whom Lucinda was betrothed; and I, too, had thought that I was without hope of comfort. But now I hear that Lucinda will not marry Fernando because she is mine, and Fernando cannot marry Lucinda because he is yours, it seems to me that there is yet some consolation for both of us. And I vow, on the faith of a gentleman, not to forsake you until I see you in the possession of Don Fernando.'

THE MEETING OF
DOROTHEA & DON QUIXOTE.

The Curate now told them both the nature of his errand, and begged that they would join him in his travels, and stay as long as they pleased at his village. By this time they heard the voice of Sancho Panza, who, not finding them where he had left them, was calling out as loudly as he might.

They went to meet him, and asked for Don Quixote. Sancho told them that he had found him almost naked to his shirt, lean and yellow, half dead with hunger, and sighing for the Lady Dulcinea; and although he had told him that she commanded him to journey to Toboso, yet he declared that he had made up his mind not to appear before her until he had done feats worthy of her great beauty.

The Curate now returned and told Dorothea of their plan, and she at once offered to act the part of the distressed damsel, for she had a lady's dress in the bundle which she carried.

'The sooner, then, we set about our work the better,' said the Barber.

Dorothea retired to put on her robe of a fine rich woollen cloth, a short mantle of another green stuff, and a collar and many rich jewels which she took from a little casket. With these things she adorned herself so gorgeously that she appeared to be a Princess at least. When Sancho saw her he was amazed, and asked the Curate with great eagerness to tell him who the lady was, and what she was doing in these out of the way places.

'This beautiful lady, brother Sancho,' replied the Curate, 'is the heiress in direct line of the mighty Kingdom of Micomicon, who has come in search of thy Master, to ask of him a boon, which is to avenge her of a wrong done by a wicked Giant. And, owing to the great fame of thy Master which has spread through all lands, this beautiful Princess has come to find him out.'

'A happy searcher and a happy finding,' cried Sancho; 'my Master shall soon slay the great lubber of a Giant, unless he turn out to be a phantom, for he has no power over those things. And when this is done, my Lord shall marry the Princess, whose name, by the bye, you have not yet told me, and by this means shall he become an Emperor, and have Islands to give away.'

'Her name,' replied the Curate, 'is the Princess Micomicona, and as to your Master's marriage, I will do what I can to help.'

Sancho was quite satisfied with these answers, and, when Dorothea had mounted the mule, he guided them towards the spot where Don Quixote was to be found. And as they went along, the Barber told Sancho he must in no way pretend to know who he was, for if he did, Don Quixote would never leave the mountains and would never become an Emperor. The Curate and Cardenio remained behind, promising to join them again on the first opportunity.

Having travelled about three-quarters of a league, they found Don Quixote clothed, though still unarmed,

sitting amidst the rocks. No sooner did Sancho tell
Dorothea that this was his Master than she whipped up
her palfrey, closely followed by the well-bearded Barber,
who jumped from his mule, and ran to help his lady
alight.

Quickly dismounting, she threw herself on her knees
before Don Quixote, and refusing his efforts to raise her,
spoke as follows: 'Never will I rise from this position,
most valiant and invincible Knight, until you grant me a
boon which will not only add to your honour and renown, but also assist the most injured and unfortunate
damsel that ever the sun beheld. And if the valour of
your mighty arm be equal to what I have heard of your
immortal fame, you can indeed render aid to a miserable
being who comes from a far-distant land to seek your
help.'

'Beauteous lady,' replied Don Quixote, 'I will not answer one word, nor hear a jot of your affairs, until you
rise from the ground.'

'I will not rise, my Lord,' answered the unfortunate
maiden, 'until I have obtained from you the boon I beg.'

'Dear Lady,' replied Don Quixote, 'it is granted, so
that it be not anything that touches my duty to my King,
my country, or the chosen Queen of my heart.'

'Your kindness shall in no way affect them,' replied
Dorothea.

At this moment Sancho came up and whispered softly
in his Master's ear: 'Sir, you may very well grant the re-

quest she asketh, for it is a mere nothing; it is only to kill a monstrous Giant, and she that demands it is the Princess Micomicona, Queen of the great Kingdom of Micomicon in Ethiopia.'

'Let her be what she will,' said Don Quixote, 'I will do my duty towards her.' And then turning to the damsel, he said: 'Rise, most beautiful Lady, for I grant you any boon you shall please to ask of me.'

'Why, then,' said Dorothea, 'what I ask of you is, that you will at once come away with me to the place where I shall guide you, and that you promise me not to undertake any new adventure, until you have revenged me on a traitor who has driven me out of my Kingdom.'

'I grant your request,' said Don Quixote, 'and therefore, Lady, you may cast away from this day forward all the melancholy that troubles you, for this mighty arm shall restore you to your Kingdom.'

The distressed damsel strove with much ado to kiss his hand, but Don Quixote, who was a most curious Knight, would not permit it, and, making her arise, treated her with the greatest respect.

He now commanded Sancho to saddle Rozinante and help him to arm himself, and this done the Knight was ready to depart. The Barber, who had been kneeling all the while, had great difficulty to stop laughing aloud at all this, and his beard was in danger of falling off. He was glad to get up and help his Lady to mount the mule, and when Don Quixote was mounted, and the Barber himself had got upon his beast, they were ready to start. As for Sancho, who trudged along on foot, he could not help grieving for the loss of his Dapple; but he bore it all with patience, for now he saw his Master on the way to marry a Princess, and so become at least King of Micomicon, though it grieved him to think that that country was peopled by blackmoors, and that when he became a ruler his vassals would all be black.

While this was going on, the Curate and Cardenio had not been idle. For the Curate was a cunning plotter, and had hit on a bright idea. He took from his pocket a pair of scissors, and cut off Cardenio's rugged beard and trimmed his hair very cleverly. And when he had thrown his riding-cloak over Cardenio's shoulders, he was so unlike what he was before, that he would not have known himself in a looking-glass. This finished, they went out to meet Don Quixote and the others.

When they came towards them, the Curate looked earnestly at the Knight for some time, and then ran towards him with open arms, saying: 'In a good hour is this meeting with my worthy countryman, the mirror of Knighthood, Don Quixote of the Mancha, the Champion of the distressed.'

Don Quixote did not at first know him, but when he remembered the Curate he wanted to alight, saying: 'It is not seemly, reverend Sir, that I should ride whilst you travel on foot.'

But the Curate would not allow him to dismount and

give him his horse, but suggested that he might ride behind the lady's Squire on his mule.

'I did not think of that, good Master Curate,' said Don Quixote; 'but I know my Lady the Princess will for my sake order her Squire to lend you the use of his saddle.'

'That I will,' said the Princess; 'and I know my Squire is the last man to grudge a share of his beast to this reverend Father.

'That is most certain,' said the Barber, and got off his steed at once.

The Curate now mounted, but the misfortune was that when the Barber tried to get up behind, the mule, which was a hired one, lifted up her legs and kicked out with such fury that she knocked Mr. Nicholas to the ground, and, as he rolled over, his beard fell off and lay upon the earth. Don Quixote, seeing that huge mass of beard torn from the jaw without blood, and lying at a distance from the Squire's face, said: 'This, I vow, is one of the greatest miracles I ever saw in my life. The beard is taken off as clean by the heel of the mule as if it had been done by the hand of a barber.'

The Curate, seeing the risk they ran of their plan being found out, came to where Master Nicholas was lying, and with one jerk clapped it on again, muttering as he did so some Latin words, which he said were a charm for fixing on beards.

By this means, to Don Quixote's amazement, the Squire was cured again, and he asked the Curate to tell him this charm, which, he said, since it could heal a

wound of this kind, must be good for even more dangerous injuries.

The Curate agreed to tell him the secret some other
day, and, having mounted the mule, the party rode
slowly away towards the Inn.

SANCHO·PANZA
RECOVERS·HIS·
D'APPLE·

CHAPTER XXI

Of the Journey to the Inn

THE Curate rode first on the mule, and with him rode Don Quixote and the Princess. The others, Cardenio, the Barber, and Sancho Panza, followed on foot.

And as they rode, Don Quixote said to the damsel: 'Madam, let me entreat your Highness to lead the way that most pleaseth you.'

Before she could answer, the Curate said: 'Towards what Kingdoms would you travel? Are you for your native land of Micomicon?'

She, who knew very well what to answer, being no babe, replied: 'Yes, Sir, my way lies towards that Kingdom.'

'If it be so,' said the Curate, 'you must pass through the village where I dwell, and from thence your Ladyship must take the road to Carthagena, where you may embark. And, if you have a prosperous journey, you may come within the space of nine years to the Lake Meona, I mean Meolidas, which stands on this side of your Highness's Kingdom some hundred days' journey or more.'

'You are mistaken, good Sir,' said she, 'for it is not yet fully two years since I left there, and, though I never had fair weather, I have arrived in time to see what I so longed for, the presence of the renowned Don Quixote of the Mancha, whose glory was known to me as soon as my foot touched the shores of Spain.'

'No more,' cried Don Quixote. 'I cannot abide to hear myself praised, for I am a sworn enemy to flattery. And though I know what you speak is but truth, yet it offends mine ears. And I can tell you this, at least, that whether I have valour or not, I will use it in your service even to the loss of my life. But let me know, Master Curate, what has brought you here?'

'You must know, then,' replied the Curate, 'that Master Nicholas, the Barber, and myself travelled towards Seville to recover certain sums of money which a kinsman of mine in the Indies had sent me. And passing yesterday through this way we were set upon by four robbers, who took everything that we had. And it is said about here, that those who robbed us were certain galley slaves, who they say were set at liberty, almost on this very spot, by a man so valiant that in spite of the guard he released them all. And doubtless he must be out of his wits, or else he must be as great a knave as they, to loose the wolf among the sheep, and rebel against his King by taking from the galleys their lawful prey.'

Sancho had told the Curate of the adventure with the galley slaves, and the Curate spoke of it to see what Don Quixote would say. The Knight, however, durst not confess his part in the adventure, but rode on, changing colour at every word the Curate spoke.

When the Curate had finished, Sancho burst out: 'By my father, Master Curate, he that did that deed was my Master, and that not for wanting of warning for I told him beforehand that it was a sin to deliver them, and that they were great rogues who had been sent to the galleys to punish them for their crimes.'

'You bottlehead!' replied Don Quixote. 'It is not the duty of Knights Errant to examine whether the afflicted, enslaved, and oppressed whom they meet by the way are in sorrow for their own default; they must relieve them because they are needy and in distress, looking at their sorrow and not at their crimes. And if any but the holy Master Curate shall find fault with me on this account, I will tell him that he knows nought of Knighthood, and that he lies in his throat, and this I will make him know by the power of my sword.'

Dorothea, who was discreet enough to see they were carrying the jest too far, now said: 'Remember, Sir Knight, the boon you promised me, never to engage in any other adventure, be it ever so urgent, until you have seen me righted. And had Master Curate known that it was the mighty arm of Don Quixote that freed the galley slaves, I feel sure he would have bit his tongue through ere he spoke words which might cause you anger.'

'That I dare swear,' said the Curate.

'Madam,' replied Don Quixote, 'I will hold my peace and keep my anger to myself, and will ride on peaceably and quietly until I have done the thing I promised. Tell me, therefore, without delay, what are your troubles and on whom am I to take revenge.'

To this Dorothea replied: 'Willingly will I do what you ask, so you will give me your attention.'

At this Cardenio and the Barber drew near to hear the witty Dorothea tell her tale, and Sancho, who was as much deceived as his Master, was the most eager of all to listen.

She, after settling herself in her saddle, began with a lively air to speak as follows: 'In the first place, I would have you know, gentlemen, that my name is——' Here she stopped a moment, for she had forgotten what name the Curate had given her.

He, seeing her trouble, said quickly: 'It is no wonder, great Lady, that you hesitate to tell your misfortunes. Great sufferers often lose their memory, so that they even forget their own names, as seems to have happened to your Ladyship, who has forgotten that she is called the Princess Micomicona, heiress of the great Kingdoms of Micomicon.'

'True,' said the damsel, 'but let me proceed. The King, my father, was called Tinacrio the Sage, and was learned in the magic art. By this he discovered that my mother, the Queen Xaramilla, would die before him, and that I should soon afterwards be left an orphan. This did not trouble him so much as the knowledge that a certain Giant, called Pandafilando of the Sour Face, Lord of a great Island near our border, when he should hear that I was an orphan, would pass over with a mighty force into my Kingdom and take it from me. My father warned me that when this came to pass I should not stay to defend myself, and so cause the slaughter of my people, but should at once set out for Spain, where I should meet with a Knight whose fame would then extend through all that Kingdom. His name, he said, should be Don Quixote, and he would be tall of stature, have a withered face, and on his right side, a little under his left shoulder, he should have a tawny spot with certain hairs like bristles.'

On hearing this, Don Quixote said: 'Hold my horse, son Sancho, and help me to strip, for I would know if I am the Knight of whom the sage King spoke.'

'There is no need,' said Sancho, 'for I know that your Worship has such a mark near your backbone.'

'It is enough,' said Dorothea, 'for among friends we must not be too particular, and whether it is on your shoulder or your backbone is of no importance. And indeed, no sooner did I land in Osuna that I heard of Don Quixote's fame, and felt sure that he was the man.'

'But how did you land in Osuna, Madam,' asked Don Quixote, 'seeing that it is not a sea town?'

'Sir,' said the Curate, 'the Princess would say that she landed at Malaga, and that Osuna was the first place wherein she heard tidings of your Worship.'

'That is so,' said Dorothea; 'and now nothing remains but to guide you to Pandafilando of the Sour Face, that I may see you slay him, and once again enter into my Kingdom. For all must succeed as the wise Tinacrio, my father, has foretold, and if the Knight of the prophecy, when he has killed the Giant, so desires, then it will be my lot to become his wife, and he will at once possess both me and my Kingdom.'

'What thinkest thou of this, friend Sancho? Did I not tell thee this would come about? Here we have a Kingdom to command and a Queen to marry.'

When Sancho heard all this he jumped for joy, and running to Dorothea stopped her mule, and asking her very humbly to give him her hand to kiss, he kneeled down as a sign that he accepted her as his Queen and Lady.

All around could scarcely hide their laughter at the Knight's madness and the Squire's simplicity, and when Dorothea promised Sancho to make him a great lord, and Sancho gave her thanks, it roused their mirth anew.

'Madam,' continued Don Quixote, who appeared to be full of thought, 'I repeat all I have said, and make my vow anew, and when I have cut off the head of Pandafilando I will put you in peaceable possession of your Kingdom, but since my memory and will are captive to another, it is not possible for me to marry.'

So disgusted was Sancho with what he heard that he cried out in a great rage: 'Surely, Sir Don Quixote, your Worship is not in your right senses. Is it possible your Worship can refuse to marry a Princess like this? A poor chance have I of getting a Countship if your Worship goes on like this, searching for mushrooms at the bottom of the sea. Is my Lady Dulcinea more beautiful? She cannot hold a candle to her. Marry her! Marry at once, and when you are King make me a Governor.'

Don Quixote, who heard such evil things spoken of his Lady Dulcinea, could not bear them any longer, and therefore, lifting up his lance, without speaking a word to Sancho, gave him two blows that brought him to the earth, and if Dorothea had not called to the Knight to spare him, without doubt he would have taken his Squire's life.

'Think you, miserable villain,' cried Don Quixote, 'that it is to be all sinning on thy side and pardoning on mine? Say, scoffer with the viper's tongue, who dost thou think hath gained this Kingdom and cut off the head of this Giant and made thee Marquis—for all this I take to be a thing as good as completed—unless it be the worth and valour of Dulcinea using my arm as her instrument? She fights in my person, and I live and breathe in her. From her I hold my life and being. O villain, how ungrateful art thou that seest thyself raised from the dust of the earth to be a nobleman, and speakest evil of her who gives thee such honours!'

Sancho was not too much hurt to hear what his Master said. He jumped up nimbly and ran behind Dorothea's palfrey, and from there said to his Master: 'Tell me, your Worship, if you are not going to marry this great Princess, how this Kingdom will become yours, and how you can do me any favours. Pray marry this Queen now we have her here. I say nothing against Lady Dulcinea's beauty, for I have never seen her.'

'How, thou wicked traitor, thou hast not seen her!' cried Don Quixote. 'Didst thou not but now bring me a message from her?'

'I mean,' replied Sancho, 'not seen her for long enough to judge of her beauty, though, from what I did see, she appeared very lovely.'

'Ah!' said Don Quixote, 'then I do excuse thee, but have a care what thou sayest, for, remember, the pitcher may go once too often to the well.'

'No more of this,' said Dorothea. 'Run, Sancho, kiss your Master's hand, and ask his pardon. Henceforth speak no evil of the Lady Dulcinea, and trust that fortune may find you an estate where you may live like a Prince.'

Sancho went up hanging his head and asked his Lord's hand, which he gave him with a grave air, and, after he had kissed it, the Knight gave him his blessing, and no more was said about it.

While this was passing, they saw coming along the road on which they were a man riding upon an Ass, and when he drew near he seemed to be a gipsy. But Sancho Panza, whenever he met with any asses, followed them with his eyes and his heart, and he had hardly caught sight of the man when he knew him to be the escaped robber, Gines of Passamonte, and the Ass to be none other than his beloved Dapple.

Gines had disguised himself as a gipsy, but Sancho knew him, and called out in a loud voice: 'Ah! thief

Gines, give up my jewel, let go my life, give up mine Ass, give up the comfort of my home. Fly, scoundrel! Begone thief! Give back what is none of thine.'

He need not have used so many words, for Gines leaped off at the first and raced away from them all as fast as his legs could carry him.

Sancho then ran up to Dapple, and, embracing him, cried: 'How hast thou been cared for, my darling and treasure, Dapple of mine eyes, my sweet companion?' With this he stroked and kissed him as if he had been a human being. But the Ass held his peace, and allowed Sancho to kiss and cherish him without answering a word.

SANCHO'S STORY
OF HIS VISIT TO
THE LADY DULCINEA

CHAPTER XXII

The Story Sancho Panzo told his Master of his
Visit to the Lady Dulcinea

WHEN the rest came up they all congratulated Sancho
on finding his ass, and Don Quixote promised that he
would still give him the three ass-colts, for which Sancho
thanked him heartily.

While the Knight and his Squire rode on ahead, the
Curate said to Cardenio: 'Is it not marvellous to see the
strange way in which this good gentleman believes all
these inventions, and this only because they wear the
style and fashion of the follies he is so fond of
reading?'

177

'It is so,' said Cardenio, 'and indeed, if he were a character in a story-book no one would believe in him.'

'There is another thing, too,' said the Curate, 'that apart from his folly about Knighthood, no one would esteem him to be other than a man of excellent judgment.'

Don Quixote at the same time was saying to Sancho:

'Friend Sancho, let us bury all injuries, and tell me when, how, and where didst thou find Dulcinea. What was she doing? What saidst thou to her? What answer made she? How did she look when she read my letter? Who copied it for thee? Tell me all, without adding to it or lying, for I would know everything.'

'Master,' replied Sancho, 'if I must speak the truth, nobody copied out the letter, for I carried no letter at all.'

'Thou sayest true,' said Don Quixote, 'for I found the pocket-book, wherein it was written, two days after thy departure, and I did expect that thou wouldst return for it.'

'I had done so,' said Sancho, 'if I had not carried it in my memory when you read it to me, so that I could say it to a parish clerk, who copied it out of my head, word for word, so exactly that he said that in all the days of his life he had never read such a pretty letter.'

'And hast thou it still by heart, Sancho?' asked Don Quixote.

'No, Sir, for after I gave it, seeing that it was to be of no more use, I let myself forget it. If I remember, it

began, *Scrubby Queen, Sovereign Lady,* and the ending
—*yours till death, the Knight of the Rueful Countenance*
—but between these things I put in three hundred *hearts,*
and *loves,* and *dear eyes.*'

'All this I like to hear, therefore say on,' said Don Quixote. 'Thou didst arrive; and what was the Queen of
Beauty doing then? I daresay thou foundest her thread-
ing pearls or embroidering some curious device, with
golden threads for this her captive Knight.'

'No, that I did not,' said Sancho, 'but winnowing two
bushels of wheat in the yard of her house.'

'Why then,' said Don Quixote, 'thou mayest reckon
that each grain of wheat was a pearl, seeing they were
touched by her hands. But tell me, when thou didst
deliver my letter, did she kiss it? Did she use any ceremony worthy of such a letter? Or what did she?'

'When I went to give it to her,' said Sancho, 'she was
all in a bustle with a good lot of wheat in her sieve, and
said to me: "Lay down that letter there on the sack, for
I cannot read it until I have winnowed all that is
here."'

'O discreet Lady!' said Don Quixote; 'she must have
done that, so that she might read and enjoy it at leisure.
Go on, then, Sancho, and tell all she said about me, and
what thou saidst to her.'

'She asked me nothing,' replied the Squire, 'but I told
her the state which I left you in for her sake, doing penance all naked from the girdle up among these rocks like
a brute beast, and I told her how you slept on the ground

and never combed your beard, but spent your time weeping and cursing your fortune.'

'There thou saidst ill,' said Don Quixote, 'for I do not curse my fortune, but rather bless it, seeing that it hath made me worthy to merit the love of so beautiful a lady as Dulcinea of Toboso. But tell me, after she had sifted her corn and sent it to the mill, did she then read my letter?'

'The letter,' replied Sancho, 'she did never read, for she said she could neither read nor write, and therefore she tore it into small pieces, and would allow no one to read it lest the whole village might know her secrets. Lastly, she told me that I was to say to your Worship that she kissed your hands, and that she had a greater desire to see you than to write to you. Therefore she begged, as you loved her, that you should quit these bushes and brambles, and leave off these mad pranks, and set out for Toboso, for she had a great longing to see your Worship. She laughed a good deal when I told her they called your Worship the Knight of the Rueful Countenance. I asked her whether the beaten Biscayan came there. She said yes, and that he was a very good fellow. I asked also after the galley slaves; but she told me that she had seen none of them as yet.'

'All goes well, then,' said Don Quixote; 'but tell me, what jewel did she bestow on thee at thy departure for reward of the tidings thou hast brought? For it is a usual and ancient custom among Knights Errant and their Ladies to give to their Squires, damsels, or dwarfs who bring good tidings, some rich jewel as a reward for their welcome news.'

'It may well be,' replied Sancho; 'and I think it was a most excellent custom, but I doubt if it exists nowadays, for it would seem to be the manner of our age only to give a piece of bread and cheese; for this was all that my Lady Dulcinea bestowed on me when I took my leave, and, by the way, the cheese was made of sheep's milk.'

'She is marvellous liberal,' said the Knight; 'and if she gave thee not a jewel of gold, it was doubtless because she had none then about her. But that will be put right some day. Knowest thou, Sancho, at what I am astonished? It is at thy sudden return, for it seems to me thou wast gone and hast come back again in the air, for thou hast been away but a little more than three days, although Toboso is more than thirty leagues from hence. Therefore I do believe that the wise Enchanter who takes care of my affairs and is my friend, must have helped thee to travel without thy being aware of it. For there are sages that take up a Knight Errant sleeping in his bed, and, without knowing how or in what manner, he wakes the next day more than a thousand leagues from the place where he fell asleep. For otherwise Knights Errant could not help one another in perils as they do now. For it may be that one is fighting in the mountains of Armenia with some dragon or fierce serpent, and is at the point of death, and, just when he least expects it, he sees on a cloud, or in a chariot of fire, some other Knight, his friend, who a little before was in England, who helps him and delivers him from danger. And all this is done by the craft and wisdom of those sage Enchanters who take care of valorous Knights. But, leaving all this apart, what dost thou think I should do about my Lady's commands to go and see her?'

'Tell me, good your Worship,' replied Sancho, 'do you intend to journey to Toboso and lose so rich and noble a prize as this Princess? Peace! take my advice and marry her in the first village that hath a parish priest, or let the Curate do it, for he is here, and remember the old saying, "A bird in the hand is worth two in the bush."'

'Look you, Sancho,' said his Master, 'if you counsel me to marry, to the end that I may be King when I have slain the Giant and be able to give you an Island, know that I can do that without marrying, for I will make it a condition that upon conquering this monster they shall give me a portion of the Kingdom, although I marry not the Princess, and this I will bestow upon thee.'

'Let it be so, then,' said Sancho. 'And trouble not your mind, I pray you, to go and see the Lady Dulcinea at this moment, but go away and kill the Giant and let us finish off this job, for I believe it will prove of great honour and greater profit.'

'I believe, Sancho,' said Don Quixote, 'that thou art in the right, and I will follow thy advice in going first with the Princess rather than visiting Dulcinea.'

At this moment Master Nicholas the Barber called out to them to stay awhile, for they wished to halt and drink at a small spring hard by. Don Quixote stopped, to Sancho's very great content, as he was already tired of telling so many lies, and feared that his Master would entrap him in his own words. For although he knew that Dulcinea was a peasant lass of Toboso, yet he had never seen her in all his life.

ANDREW SALUTES
DON QUIXOTE

CHAPTER XXIII

What happened during their further Journey
towards the Inn

THEY all dismounted at the spring, and by this time Cardenio had dressed himself in the boy's clothes that Dorothea had worn, which, though by no means good, were better than those he cast off. The Curate had brought some scanty provisions from the Inn, and they sat down near the spring to satisfy, as well as they could, the hunger they all felt.

Whilst they took their ease, a young lad passed by, who looked very earnestly at all those what sat round the spring, and after a moment ran up to Don Quixote and embracing his legs, burst into tears, crying: 'Ah, my

184

Lord, do not you know me? Look well upon me. I am the boy Andrew whom you unloosed from the oak-tree to which I was tied.'

Don Quixote knew him at once, and, taking him by the hand, turned to those who were present and said: 'That you may see how important it is to have Knights Errant in the world to set right the wrongs and injuries which are done by insolent and wicked men, you must know that a few days ago, as I rode through a wood, I heard piteous screams and cries as of some person in sore distress. I hastened instantly to the place, and there I found tied to an oak this boy whom you see here, and I am glad that he is here, because if I shall not say the truth, he may check me. He was tied to an oak-tree, stark naked from the waist upward, and a certain clown, whom I afterwards learned to be his master, was beating him with a horse's bridle. As soon as I saw him I asked the master the reason of his cruelty. The Farmer replied that he was beating him because he was his servant, and that he had been guilty of carelessness due rather to knavery than stupidity. At which the lad said, "Sir, he beats me only because I ask him for my wages." The Farmer answered with many excuses, which I heard but did not believe. I made him at once untie the boy, and forced him to swear me an oath that he would take him home with him and pay him every *real* upon the nail. Is not all this true, son Andrew? Answer, nor hestiate in anything. Tell these gentlemen what passed, that they may learn how necessary it is to have Knights Errant up and down the highways.'

'All that your Worship says is very true,' replied the lad; 'but the end of the business was very contrary to what you imagine.'

'How contrary?' asked Don Quixote. 'Did not the clown pay thee, then?'

'He not only did not pay me,' answered the boy, 'but as soon as you had passed out of the wood, and we were alone again, he tied me to the same tree and gave me afresh so many blows that I had like to be flayed alive. And at each blow he uttered some jest to make a mock of your Lordship, and if I had not felt so much pain, I could have found it in my heart to have laughed very merrily. In fact, he left me in such a wretched plight that I have been in hospital ever since. And you are at fault in all this, for if you had ridden on your way, and not come meddling in other folk's affairs, perhaps my master would have contented himself with giving me a dozen blows or so, and would presently have let me loose and paid me my wages. But, because you abused him so harshly, his anger was aroused, and as he could not revenge himself on you, as soon as he was alone he let loose the storm of his wrath upon me, in such a manner that I fear I shall never be a man again as long as I live.'

'The mischief was,' said Don Quixote, 'in my going away, for I should not have departed until I had seen thee paid. For I might well have known that no churl will keep his word if he finds that it does not suit him to keep it. But yet, Andrew, thou dost remember how I swort that if he paid thee not, I would return and seek him out, and find him though he should hide himself in the belly of a whale.'

'That is true,' replied Andrew, 'but it is all of no use.'

'Thou shalt see whether it is of use or no presently,' said Don Quixote, and so saying he got up hastily and commanded Sancho to bridle Rozinante, who was feeding whilst they did eat.

Dorothea asked him what it was he meant to do. He answered that he meant to go in search of the Farmer and punish him for his bad conduct, and make him pay Andrew to the last farthing, in spite of all the churls in the world. To which she answered, entreating him to remember that he could not deal with any other adventure, according to his promise, until he had finished hers; and as he knew this better than any one else, he must restrain his anger until he returned from her Kingdom.

'That is true,' answered Don Quixote; 'and Andrew must have patience until my return, for I once more vow and promise anew never to rest until he be satisfied and paid.'

'I do not believe these vows,' said Andrew; 'I would rather just now have as much money as would help me on my way to Seville than all the revenge in the world. Give me something to eat, and let me go, and may all Knights Errant be as erring to themselves as they have been with me.'

Sancho took out of his bag a piece of bread and cheese, and, giving it to the lad, said: 'Take it, brother Andrew, for each of us has a share in your misfortune.'

'What share have you in it?' asked Andrew.

'This piece of bread and cheese which I give thee,' said Sancho, 'for no one knows whether I shall have need of it again or not. For you must know, my friend, that we Squires to Knights Errant suffer great hunger and ill-luck, and many things which are better felt than told.'

Andrew laid hold of his bread and cheese, and, seeing that no one gave him anything else, bowed his head and went on his way. And as he went he turned to Don Quixote and said: 'I pray you, Sir Knight Errant, if you meet me again, although you should see me being cut to pieces, do not come to my aid, but leave me to my ill fate. For it cannot be so great but that greater will result from your help, and may you and all the Knights Errant that ever were born in the world keep your paths away from mine.'

Don Quixote started up to chastise him, but he set off running so fast that no one tried to pursue him. The Knight was greatly ashamed at Andrew's story, and the others had much ado not to laugh outright, and so put him to utter confusion.

When they had finished their dinner, they saddled and went to horse once more, and travelled all that day and the next without any adventure of note, until they arrived at the Inn, which was the dread and terror of Sancho Panza, and though he would rather not have entered it, yet he could not avoid doing so. The Inn-keeper, the Hostess, her daughter, and Maritornes, seeing Don Quixote and Sancho return, went out to meet them with tokens of great love and joy. The Knight returned their compliments with grave courtesy and bade them prepare a better bed than they gave him the last time.

'Sir,' said the Hostess, 'if you would pay us better than the last time, we would give you one fit for a Prince.'

Don Quixote answered that he would, and they prepared a reasonable good bed for him in the same room where he lay before. Then he went off to bed at once, because he was tired and weary, both in body and mind.

He had scarcely locked himself in, when the Hostess ran at the Barber, seizing him by the beard, and cried: 'By my troth, but my tail shall no longer be used for a beard, for the comb which used to be kept in the tail gets tossed about the floor, and it is a shame.'

But the Barber would not give it up for all her tugging, until the Curate told him to let her have it, for there was no longer any need of a disguise, as the Barber might now appear in his own shape, and tell Don Quixote that after he had been robbed by the galley slaves he had fled for refuge to that Inn. As for the Princess's Squire, if the Knight should ask after him, they could say he had been sent on before to her Kingdom, to announce to her subjects that she was returning, bringing with her one who should give them all their freedom. On this the Barber gave up the tail to the landlady, together with the other things they had borrowed.

All the people of the Inn were struck with Dorothea's beauty and the comeliness of the shepherd Cardenio. The Curate made them get ready a dinner of the best the Inn could produce, and the Innkeeper, in hope of better payment, prepared them very speedily a good dinner. All this was done whilst Don Quixote slept, and they agreed not to wake him, for they thought it would do him more good to sleep than to eat.

DON QUIXOTE'S
EXTRAORDINARY BATTLE

CHAPTER XXIV

Of the extraordinary Battle which Don Quixote
waged with what he took to be a Giant

DON QUIXOTE was still asleep when the dinner was
served, and during dinner—the Innkeeper, his wife, his
daughter, and Maritornes being there, as well as all the
travellers—they talked of Don Quixote's strange craze,
and of the state in which they had found him. The Hostess told them of what had happened between him and
the Carrier, and glancing round to see if Sancho were
present, and not seeing him, she told them the story of
his being tossed in the blanket, to the no small entertainment of all the company.

The Curate told him it was the books of Knighthood
that Don Quixote had read that had turned his head.

'I know not how that can be,' said the Innkeeper, 'for
to my thinking there is no finer reading in the world; and
when it is harvest-time, the reapers here often collect
during the midday heat, and one who can read takes one
of these books in hand, while some thirty of us get round
him, and sit listening with so much delight that I could
find it in my heart to be hearing such stories day and
night.'

'And I think well of them, too,' said the Hostess, 'for when the reading is going on, you are so full of it that you forget to scold me, and I have a good time of it.'

'Ah,' said her daughter, 'I too listen, and though I like not the fights which please my father, yet the lamentations which the Knights make when they are away from their Ladies make me weep for pity, and I enjoy that.'

'We have need here,' said the Curate, 'of our friends, the old woman and the Niece. Beware, my good Host, of these books, and take care that they carry you not on the road they have taken Don Quixote.'

'Not so,' said the Innkeeper, 'I shall not be such a fool as to turn Knight Errant; for I see well enough that it is not the fashion now to do as they used to do in the times when these famous Knights roamed about the world. All that is of no use nowadays.'

Sancho came in in the midst of this, and was amazed to hear them say that Knights Errant now were of no use, and that books of Knighthood were full of follies and lies, and he made up his mind to see the end of this voyage of his Master, and if that did not turn out as happily as he expected, to return home to his wife and children and to his former labours.

At this moment a noise came from the room where Don Quixote was lying, and Sancho went hastily to see if his Master wanted anything.

In a few moments he returned, rushing wildly back, and shouting at the top of his voice: 'Come, good Sirs, quickly, and help my Master, who is engaged in one of the most terrible battles my eyes have ever seen. I swear he has given the Giant, the enemy of my Lady, the Princess Micomicona, such a cut, that he has sliced his head clean off like a turnip.'

'What sayest thou, friend?' said the Curate. 'Art thou in thy wits, Sancho? How can it be as you say, when the Giant is at least two thousand leagues from here?'

By this time they heard a marvellous great noise within the chamber, and Don Quixote shouting out: 'Hold, thief, scoundrel, rogue! now I have thee, and thy scimitar shall not avail thee!'

And it seemed as if he were striking a number of mighty blows on the walls.

'Do not stand there listening,' cried Sancho, 'but go in and part the fray, or aid my Master. Though I think it will not now be necessary, for doubtless the Giant is dead by now, and giving an account of the ill life he led; for I saw his blood was all about the house and his head cut off, which is as big as a great wine-bag.'

'May I be hewed in pieces,' cried the Innkeeper on hearing this, 'if Don Quixote has not been slashing at one of the skins of red wine that are standing filled at his bed head, and the wine that is spilt must be what this fellow takes for blood.'

So saying he ran into the room, and the rest followed him, and found Don Quixote in the strangest guise imaginable. He was in his shirt, which did not reach to his knees. His legs were very long and lean, covered with hair, and not over clean. On his head he wore a greasy red nightcap which belonged to the Innkeeper. Round his left arm he had folded the blanket from off his bed, at which Sancho gazed angrily, for he owed that blanket a grudge. In his right hand he gripped his naked sword, with which he laid round about him with many a thwack, shouting out as if indeed he was at battle with some terrible Giant. The best sport of all was that his eyes were not open, for he was indeed asleep, and dreaming that he was fighting a Giant. For his imagination was so full of the adventure in front of him that he dreamed he had already arrived at Micomicon, and was there in combat with his enemy; and he had given so many blows to the wine-bags, supposing them to be the Giant, that the whole chamber flowed with wine.

When the Innkeeper saw this, he flew into such a rage that he set upon Don Quixote with his clenched fist, and began to pummel him, so that if Cardenio and the Curate had not pulled him off, he would have finished the battle of the Giant altogether. In spite of this, the poor Knight did not awake until the Barber got a great kettleful of cold water from the well, and threw it right over him, when Don Quixote woke up, but even then did not understand where he was.

As for Sancho, he went up and down the floor, searching for the Giant's head, and seeing he could not find it, said: 'Now I know that everything I see in this house is enchanted, for this head is not to be seen here, though I myself saw it cut off with my own eyes, and the blood running from the body as from a fountain.'

'What blood or what fountain dost thou cackle of here?' cried the Innkeeper. 'Thou thief! dost thou not see that the blood and the fountain is no other thing but the wine-bags which are ripped open, and the red wine which swims up and down the room?'

'I know nothing but this,' replied Sancho, 'that if I cannot find the Giant's head, my Earldom will dissolve like salt cast into water.' For indeed Sancho awake was worse than his Master asleep, so greatly had his Master's promises turned his brain.

The Innkeeper was at his wits' end at seeing the stupidity of the Squire and the mischief done by his Master, but he determined that they should not as before go away without paying; that Knighthood should be no excuse for this, and he would make them pay for the very patches in the wine-skins that had been ruined.

All this time the Curate was holding Don Quixote's hands, who, believing that he had finished the adventure and was in the presence of the Princess Micomicona herself, fell on his knees before the Curate, and said: 'Your Highness, exalted and beautiful Lady, may live from henceforth secure from any danger that this wretched Giant might have done to you; and I am also freed this day from the promise I made to you, seeing that I have, with the assistance of her through whose favour I live and breathe, so happily completed my labour.'

'Did I not say so?' cried Sancho, hearing his Master. 'I was not drunk. My Master has salted the Giant down this time, and my Earldom is secure.'

Who could help laughing at the follies of the two, Master and man? All of them laughed except the Innkeeper, who burst out into fits of anger ten times worse than before.

At length the Barber, Cardenio, and the Curate managed, not without much ado, to get Don Quixote to bed again, and presently left him sleeping, with every sign of being worn out. They let him sleep, and went out to comfort Sancho Panza, whose grief was great at not finding the Giant's head. But they had more to do to pacify the Innkeepeer, who was almost out of his wits at the sudden death of his wine-skins.

His wife, too, was running up and down, scolding and crying out: 'Alas, the unlucky hour when this Knight Errant came to my house! Would that mine eyes had never seen him, for he has cost me dear. The last time he was here he went away scot free for his supper, bed, straw, and barley for himself, his man, his horse, and his ass, because he said he was a Knight Errant. Then for his sake the other gentlemen came and took away my good tail, and have returned it damaged, and now he breaks my wine-skins and spills the wine. I wish I may see as much of his blood spilt.' And backed up by Maritornes, the good Innkeeper's wife continued her lamentations with great fury.

At length the Curate quelled the storm, promising to satisfy them for the wine and the skins, and also for the damage to the tail, about which there was so much fuss. Dorothea comforted Sancho, telling him that as soon as ever it was made certain that his Master had slain the Giant, and placed her safely in her Kingdom, she would give him the best Earldom she had.

With this he was consoled, and told her that he himself had seen the Giant's head cut off, and that it had a beard which reached down to his girdle, and that if the beard could not now be found it was because the affairs of this house were all guided by enchantment, as he knew to his cost by what had happened to himself in his last visit.

Dorothea replied that she was of the same opinion, and bade him be of good cheer, since all would be well ended to his heart's desire.

CHAPTER XXV

Which treats of other rare Adventures which
happened at the Inn

LATER in the day the Innkeeper, who was standing at the door, cried out: 'Here is a fine troop of guests coming. If they stop here, we may sing and rejoice.'

'Who are they?' asked Cardenio.

'Four men on horseback,' answered the Innkeeper, 'with lances and targets, and all with black masks on their faces. With them comes a woman dressed in white, on a side-saddle, and her face also masked, and two lackeys that run with them on foot.'

'Are they near?' asked the Curate.

'So near,' replied the Innkeeper, 'that they are now arriving.'

Hearing this, Dorothea veiled her face, and Cardenio
went into Don Quixote's room; and they had hardly time
to do this when the whole party, of whom the Innkeeper
had spoken, entered the Inn. The four who were on
horseback were of comely and gallant bearing, and, having dismounted, went to help down the Lady on the side-
saddle; and one of them, taking her in his arms, placed
her upon a chair that stood at the door of the room into
which Cardenio had entered. All this while neither she
nor they took off their masks, or said a word, only the
Lady, as she sank into the chair, breathed a deep sigh,
and let fall her arms as one who was sick and faint. The
lackeys led away the horses to the stable.

The Curate, seeing and noting all this, and curious to
know who they were that came to the Inn in such strange
attire and keeping so close a silence, went after one of
the lackeys, and asked of him what he wanted to learn.

'Faith, Sir, I cannot tell you who these are, but they
seem to be persons of good quality, especially he who
went to help the Lady dismount. The rest obey him in
all things.'

'And the Lady—who is she?' asked the Curate.

'I cannot tell you that neither,' replied the lackey, 'for
I have not once seen her face during all the journey,
though I have often heard her groan and utter deep
sighs.'

'And have you heard the name of any of them?' asked
the Curate.

'Not I, indeed,' replied the man; 'they travel in silence, and nothing is heard but the sighs and sobs of the poor Lady, and it is our firm belief that, wherever she is going, she is going against her will.'

'May be it is so,' said the Curate, and he returned to the Inn.

Dorothea, who heard the disguised Lady sigh so mournfully, moved by pity, drew near to her and asked: 'What ails you, good Madam, for I offer you my service and good-will, and would help you as much as lies in my power?'

To this the unhappy Lady made no reply; and though Dorothea again spoke kindly to her, yet she sat silent and spoke not a word.

At length the masked gentleman came across and said to Dorothea: 'Lady, do not trouble yourself to offer anything to that women; she is of a most ungrateful nature, and not wont to return any courtesy.'

'I have never spoken,' said the silent Lady, 'since I am too unhappy to do so, and am almost drowned in my misfortunes.'

Cardenio overheard these words very clearly and distinctly, for he was close to her who uttered them, the door of Don Quixote's room being the only thing that separated them, and he cried aloud: 'What is this I hear? What voice is this that hath touched mine ear?'

The Lady, moved with a sudden passion, turned her head at these cries, and as she could not see who uttered them, she rose to her feet and would have entered the room, but the gentleman stopped her and would not let her move a step.

This sudden movement loosened the mask, which fell from her face, discovering her marvellous beauty. But her countenance was wan and pale, and she turned her eyes from place to place as one distracted, which caused Dorothea and the rest to behold her with a vast pity.

The gentleman held her fast by the shoulders, and was so busied that he could not hold up his own mask, which fell from his face, and, as it did so. Dorothea looked up and discovered that it was her lover, Don Fernando.

Scarce had she known him than, breathing out a long and most pitiful 'Alas!' from the bottom of her heart, she fell backward in a swoon. And if the Barber had not been by good chance at hand, she would have fallen on the ground with all the weight of her body.

The Curate removed the veil from her face, and cast water thereon, and Don Fernando, as soon as he looked upon her, turned as pale as death. Cardenio, who had heard the moan which Dorothea uttered, as she fell fainting on the floor, came out of the room, and saw Don Fernando holding his beloved Lucinda.

All of them held their peace and beheld one another; Dorothea looking on Don Fernando, Don Fernando on Cardenio, Cardenio on Lucinda, and Lucinda on Cardenio, all stood dumb and amazed, as folk that knew not what had befallen them.

Lucinda was the first to break the silence. 'Leave me, Don Fernando,' she cried, 'for the sake of what is due to yourself. Let me cleave to the wall whose ivy I am, to his support from whom neither your threats nor your promises could part me.'

By this time Dorothea had come to herself, and seeing that Don Fernando did not release Lucinda, she arose, and casting herself at his feet, shed a flood of crystal tears as she thus addressed him: 'If the sun of Lucinda's beauty hath not blinded thine eyes, know that she who is kneeling at thy feet is the hapless and miserable Dorothea. I am that lowly country girl to whom thou didst promise marriage. Know, my dear Lord, that the matchless love I bear thee may make amends for the beauty and nobility of her for whom thou dost abandon me. Thou canst not be the beautiful Lucinda's, because thou art mine; nor she thine, for she belongs to Cardenio. And all this being so, as in truth it is, and seeing that thou art as good as thou art noble, wherefore put off making me once more happy again? Do not vex the declining years of my parents, who have ever been loyal vassals to thine. For remember, whether thou wilt or no, thou must ever remain my promised husband.'

These and many other reasons did the grieved Dorothea use, with so much feeling and so many tears, that all who were present, even those who had come with Don Fernando, could not help from giving her their sympathy.

As for Don Fernando, he stood gazing fixedly at Dorothea for some time, and at last, overwhelmed with remorse and admiration, he took her to his arms, saying: 'Thou hast vanquished, O beautiful Dorothea. Thou hast vanquished!'

At the same moment, Cardenio, who had stood close to Don Fernando, started forward to catch the fainting Lucinda, who threw both her arms around his neck, crying: 'Thou, and thou only, art my Lord and Master.'

Thus were the true lovers all united, and the good Curate, the Barber, and even Sancho Panza joined in their tears, delighted that so much joy had taken the place of so much misery. As for Sancho, he excused himself afterwards for his tears, saying he wept only because he saw that Dorothea was not the Queen of Micomicona as he had imagined, from whom he hoped to have received such mighty gifts and favours.

Each in turn told his or her story, and Don Fernando gave an account of all that had befallen him in the city, after he had found the scroll that Lucinda had written in which she declared her love for Cardenio.

And it appeared that, the day after the interruption of the wedding, Lucinda had secretly departed from her father's house, and had fled no one knew whither; but within a few months Don Fernando had learned that she was in a certain convent, intending to remain there all the days of her life, if she could not pass them with Cardenio. As soon as he had learned that, choosing three gentlemen to aid him, he went to the place where she was. One day he surprised her walking with one of the nuns in the cloisters, and carried her off without giving her a chance to resist. From there they brought her to a certain village, where they disguised themselves, and so rode on until they came to the Inn. But Lucinda, after she was in his power, did nothing but weep and sigh without speaking a word.

Thus in silence and tears had they reached this Inn, which to him and all of them would always remain the most beautiful place in the world, since it had seen the end of so many troubles, and brought him back to his own true love.

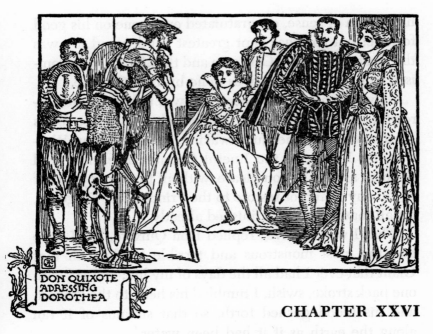

DON QUIXOTE
ADRESSING
DOROTHEA

CHAPTER XXVI

Wherein is continued the History of the
famous Princess Micomicona

SANCHO gave ear to what he heard with no small grief of mind, seeing that all hopes of his Earldom vanished away like smoke, and the fair Princess Micomicona was turned into Dorothea, whilst his Master was sound asleep, careless of all that happened. Dorothea could not believe that the happiness she enjoyed was not a dream. Cardenio and Lucinda were of a similar mind, and Don Fernando was truly thankful that he was free from the dangerous path he had taken, which must have ended in loss of all honour and credit.

In a word, all were contented and happy. The Curate,

like a man of sense, congratulated every one on his good fortune; but she that kept greatest Jubilee and joy was the Hostess, because Cardenio and the Curate had promised to pay all the damages done by Don Quixote.

Only Sancho, as has been said, was unhappy and sorrowful. And thus he went with a melancholy face to his Master, who was then just awaking, and said: 'Your Worship, Sir Knight of the Rueful Countenance, may well sleep on as long as you please, without troubling yourself to kill any Giant, or restore to the Princess her Kingdom, for all that is done and finished already.'

'That I well believe,' replied Don Quixote, 'for I have had the most monstrous and terrible battle with that Giant that ever I had all the days of my life; and yet with one back stroke, swish, I tumbled his head to the ground, and his blood gushed forth, so that streams of it ran along the earth as if it had been water.'

'As if it had been red wine, your Worship might have said,' replied Sancho, 'for I would have you know, if you do not know already, that the dead Giant is no other than a ruined wine-bag, and the blood six-and-twenty gallons of red wine.'

'What sayest thou, madman?' cried Don Quixote. 'Art thou in thy right wits?'

'Get up, Sir,' said Sancho, 'and you shall see yourself the fine piece of work you have done, and what we have to pay. You shall behold the Queen turned into a private Lady, called Dorothea, with many other things that may well astonish you.'

'I should marvel at nothing,' replied Don Quixote, 'for

if thou rememberest right, I told thee, the other time that we were here, how all that happened here was done by enchantment, and it would be no wonder if it were the same now.'

'I should believe it all,' replied Sancho, 'if my tossing in the blanket had been a thing of that sort. Only it was not so, but very real and certain. And I saw the Innkeeper, who is here to this day, hold one end of the blanket and toss me up to the sky with very good grace and strength, and as much mirth as muscle. And where it comes to knowing persons, I hold, though I may be a simpleton and a sinner, that there is no enchantment, but only bruising and bad luck.'

'Well,' cried Don Quixote, 'time will show; but give me my clothes, for I would see these wonders that thou speakest of for myself.'

Sancho gave him his clothes, and, whilst he was making him ready, the Curate told Don Fernando and the rest of Don Quixote's mad pranks, and the plan he had used to get him away from the Brown Mountains, where he imagined he was exiled through the disdain of his Lady.

The Curate told them further, that since the good fortune of the Lady Dorothea prevented them carrying out their scheme, they must invent some other way of taking him home to his village.

Cardenio offered to continue the adventure, and let Lucinda take Dorothea's part.

'No,' cried Don Fernando. 'It shall not be so, for I will have Dorothea herself carry out her plan, and if the good

Knight's home is not far from here, I shall be very glad to help in his cure.'

'It is not more than two days' journey,' said the Curate.

'Even if it were more,' replied Don Fernando, 'I should be happy to make the journey in so good a cause.'

At this moment Don Quixote sallied out, completely armed with Mambrino's helmet, which had a great hole in it, on his head, his shield on his arm, and leaning on his lance. His grotesque appearance amazed Don Fernando and his companions very much, who wondered at his gaunt face so withered and yellow, the strangeness of his arms, and his grave manner of proceeding.

All stood silent to see what he would do, whilst the Knight, casting his eyes on the beautiful Dorothea, with great gravity and calmness spoke as follows: 'I am informed, beautiful Lady, by this my Squire, that your greatness has come to an end, and your condition is destroyed. For, instead of being a Queen and a mighty Princess, you are now become a private damsel. If this has been done by the special order of that sage magician, the King your Father, because he dreaded that I could not give you all necessary help, I say that he does not know half his art, and has never understood the histories of knightly adventures. For if he had read them with the attention that I have, he would have found how many Knights of less fame than myself have ended far more desperate adventures than this, for it is no great matter to kill a Giant, be he ever so proud. For in truth it is not so many hours since I myself fought with one; but I will be silent, lest they tell me I lie. Time, the detector of all things, will disclose it when we least expect.'

'Thou foughest with two wine-bags, not with a Giant,' cried the Innkeeper.

Don Fernando told him to be silent and not to interrupt Don Quixote, who continued his speech thus: 'In fine, I say, high and disinherited Lady, do not trouble if your Father has made this change in you, for there is no peril so great on earth but my sword shall open a way through it, and by overthrowing your enemies' head to the ground I shall set your crown on your own head within a few days.'

Don Quixote said no more, but waited for the Princess's answer. She knowing Don Fernando's wish that she should continue to carry out their plan, answered with a good grace and pleasant manner, saying: 'Whosoever informed you, valorous Knight of the Rueful Countenance, that I have altered and transformed my being, hath not told you the truth, for I am the very same to-day as I was yesterday. True it is that my fortunes have somewhat changed, and given me more than I hoped for or could wish for, but for all that I have not ceased to be what I was before, and I still hope to have the aid of your valorous and invincible arm. Therefore, good my Lord, restore to my Father his honour, and believe him to be both wise and sagacious, for by his magic he has found me a remedy for all my misfortunes. For I believe that had it not been for you, I should never have attained the happiness I now enjoy, and that I speak the truth these good gentlemen will bear witness. All that is now wanted is that to-morrow morning we set out on our journey. As for the conclusion of the good success I hourly expect, that I leave to the valour of your invincible arm.'

Thus spoke the witty Dorothea, and Don Quixote, having heard her, turned to Sancho with an air of great indignation, and said: 'Now, I say unto thee, Sancho, thou art the veriest little rascal in all Spain. Tell me, thief and vagabond, didst thou not tell me that this Princess was turned into a damsel, and that she was called Dorothea? And that the head that I slashed from a Giant's shoulders, was a wine-skin, with a thousand other follies, that threw me into the greatest confusion I was ever in in my life? I vow,' he continued, looking up to the heavens and crashing his teeth together, 'I vow that I am about to make such a havoc of thee, as shall beat some wit into the pates of all the lying Squires that shall hereafter ever serve Knights Errant in this world.'

'I pray you have patience, good my Lord,' answered Sancho, 'for it may well befall me to be deceived touching the change of the Lady and Princess Micomicona. But in what touches the Giant's head, or at least the cutting of the wine-bags, and that the blood was but red wine, I am not deceived, I swear. For the bags lie wounded there at your own bed-head, and the red wine hath made a lake in your room: and all this you will know, when his honour the Landlord asks you to pay the damages.'

'I tell thee, Sancho, thou art a blockhead,' said Don Quixote. 'Pardon me, we have had enough of it.'

'Enough, indeed,' said Don Fernando, 'and let me entreat you to say no more of it. Seeing my Lady the Princess says she will go away to-morrow, as it is too late to depart to-day, let us agree to spend this evening in pleasant discourse, and to-morrow we will attend the worthy Knight Don Quixote, and be eye-witness of the valorous feats of arms he shall do in carrying out this adventure.'

It was now time for supper, and they all sat down at a long table, for there was not a square or round one in the whole house. And they gave the principal end to Don Quixote, though he did all he could to refuse it; but when he had taken it, he commanded that the Lady Micomicona should sit at his elbow as he was her champion. The others being placed in due order, they all enjoyed a pleasant supper, listening to the wise, strange discourse that Don Quixote held upon his favourite subject of knightly adventures.

CHAPTER XXVII

Of the strange Enchantment of the Unfortunate
Knight

AFTER supper it appeared that there were not sufficient rooms in the house for all the company, so the ladies retired to the best apartments, whilst the gentlemen sought rest where they could get it with the least discomfort. Sancho Panza found a bed on his Ass's harness, where he was soon fast asleep, and Don Quixote satisfied his sense of duty by arming himself, mounting Rozinante, and riding round the Inn, that he might act as sentinel of this imaginary Castle.

In a short time all the Inn was drowned in a deep sleep. Only the Innkeeper's daughter and Maritornes were not asleep, but knowing very well Don Quixote's humour, and that he was armed on horseback outside the Inn keeping guard, the two agreed to play him some trick, or at least to pass a little time listening to his nonsense.

It so happened that there was not any window in all the Inn which looked out into the fields, but only a hole in the barn, out of which they were used to throw the straw. To this hole came the two damsels, and saw Don

THE ENCHANTMENT
OF DON QUIXOTE

Quixote mounted and leaning on his lance, breathing forth ever and anon such doleful sighs, that it seemed as if each one of them would tear his very soul. They noted besides how he said in a soft and amorous voice: 'O my Lady Dulcinea of Toboso, the perfection of all beauty, the sum-total of discretion, the treasury of grace, the storehouse of virtue, the ideal of all that is worthy, modest, or delightful in all the world! What might thy Ladyship be doing at this present? Art thou perhaps thinking of thy captive Knight who most readily exposeth himself to so many dangers for thy sake? Give me tidings of her, O thou Moon! Mayhap thou dost now look down upon her pacing some gallery of her sumptuous palace, or leaning against some balcony thinking what glory she shall give me for my pains, what quiet to my cares, what life to my death, and what reward for my services. And thou, O Sun, who art even now busy saddling thy horses to set off betimes and go forth and see my Lady, I beseech thee when thou seest her to salute her on my behalf, but take care that thou dost not kiss her on her face lest thou provokest my jealousy.'

So far the Knight had proceeded when the Innkeeper's daughter began to call him softly to her, saying: 'Sir Knight, approach a little way, if you please.'

At this signal Don Quixote turned his head and saw by the light of the moon, which shined then very clearly, that they beckoned him from the hole in the barn, which he imagined to be a fair window full of iron bars gilded in costly fashion with gold, fit for so rich a Castle as he imagined that Inn to be. In a moment he believed, in his strange fancy, that the beautiful damsel, daughter to the Lord of the Castle, conquered by love of him, was come to have speech with him.

In this fancy, and because he would not show himself discourteous and ungrateful, he turned Rozinante about and came over to the hole, and then, having beheld the two damsels, he said: 'I take pity on you, beautiful Lady, that you have fixed your love where it is not possible to find another's in return. Nor must you blame this miserable Knight Errant, whom love hath wholly disabled from paying his addresses to any other than to her who at first sight became the Lady of his choice. Pardon me, therefore, good Lady, and retire yourself to your room, and be pleased to say no more to me, that I may not appear ungrateful to you. And if, of the love you bear me you can find me any other way wherein I may serve you, demand it boldly, for I swear to pleasure you in this, even though my task be to bring you a lock of Medusa's hairs, which are all of snakes, or to capture the beams of the sun in a phial of glass.'

'My Lady needs none of these things, Sir Knight,' answered Maritornes.

'What doth she then want, discreet dame?' asked Don Quixote.

'Only one of your fair hands,' said Maritornes, 'that she may fulfil the desire that brought her to this window with so great danger to herself, that if her Lord and Father knew of it, the least he would do would be to slice off her ear.'

'He had best beware of what he does,' answered Don

Quixote, 'unless he would make the most disastrous end that ever father made in this world, for having laid violent hands on the delicate limbs of his amorous daughter.'

Maritornes had no doubt but that Don Quixote would give up his hand as he was requested, and, having made up her mind what she would do, she went down into the stable, and fetched out Sancho Panza's Ass's halter. With this she returned again as quickly as possible, and came to the hole just as Don Quixote had set his feet upon Rozinante's saddle that he might the better reach the barred windows at which he thought the lovesick damsel was standing.

And as he stretched forth his hand to her he cried: 'Hold, Lady, this hand, or, as I may better say, this scourge of evildoers. Hold, I say, this hand, which no other woman ever touched before, not even she herself who holds entire possession of my whole body. Nor do I give it to you to the end that you should kiss it, but that you may behold the strength of the sinews, the knitting of the muscles, the large and swelling veins, whereby you may learn how mighty is the force of that arm to which such a hand is knit.'

'We shall see that presently,' said Maritornes.

And then, making a running knot in the halter, she cast it on the wrist of his hand, and, coming down from the hole, she tied the other end of the halter very fast to the bolt of the hay-loft door.

Don Quixote, feeling the roughness of the halter about his wrist, said: 'It seems that you rather rasp than clasp my hand, but yet I pray you not to handle it so roughly,

seeing it is in no fault for what you suffer from my incli-
nations. Remember that those who love well do not take
so cruel revenge on those who love elsewhere.'

But nobody gave ear to those words of Don Quixote.
For, as soon as Maritornes had tied him fast, she and the
other, almost bursting with laughter, ran away and left
him fastened in such a manner that it was not possible
for him to loose himself. He was standing, as has been
said, on Rozinante's saddle, with his whole arm thrust
within the hole, and fastened to the bolt of the door, and
was in great fear that if Rozinante budged never so little
on either side he should fall and hang by the arm. Therefore he durst not make the least movement, though he
might have expected, from Rozinante's patience and mild
spirit, that if he were allowed, he would stand without
stirring for a whole century.

In fine, Don Quixote, finding that he was tied up and
that the ladies were gone, began at once to imagine that
all this had been done by way of enchantment, as the
time before when he and Sancho had suffered such
strange adventures. Then he was wroth with himself for
his want of judgment and discretion in venturing to enter
the Castle a second time, seeing that he had come off so
badly the first. For it was a maxim with the Knights Errant, that when they had attempted an adventure and
had not come well out of it, it was a token that it was not
reserved for them but for some other.

Yet for all this he drew forward his arm to see if he
might deliver himself, but he was so well bound that all
his efforts proved vain. It is true that he drew his arm

cautiously, lest Rozinante should stir, and though he longed to get into the seat of his saddle again, yet he could do no other but stand upright or wrench off his arm. Many times did he wish for the sword of Amadis against which no enchantment had power. Then he fell to cursing his stars, or again called upon the Lady Dulcinea to remember him anew. Now he would call on his good Squire Sancho Panza, who, buried in sleep, stretched out upon his pack-saddle, heard him not, and then he called in vain on the Sage Urganda to release him.

Finally, the morning found him so full of despair and confusion, that he roared like a bull, for he had no hope that daylight would bring him any cure, as he fully believed his enchantment would prove ever lasting. This belief was strengthened inasmuch as Rozinante had not budged ever so little, and he came to the conclusion that both he and his horse should abide in that state without eating, drinking, or sleeping, until either the evil influences of the stars were passed, or some great Enchanter had disenchanted him.

In this he was deceived, for scarce did day begin to peep than there arrived four horsemen at the Inn door, with firelocks on their saddle-bows, who were officers of the Holy Brotherhood. They called out at the Inn door, which was still shut, giving loud knocks, which, being heard by Don Quixote from the place where he stood sentinel, he cried out in a loud and arrogant voice: 'Knights or Squires, or whatsoever else ye be, you are not to knock any more at the gates of this Castle, seeing that at such an hour as this either those who are within are sleeping, or else are not wont to open their fortress until Phœbus hath spread his beams over the earth. Therefore stand back and wait until it be clear day, and then we will see whether it be just or no, that they should open their gates unto you.'

'What Castle or Fortress is this,' cried one of them, 'that we should observe these ceremonies? If thou beest the Innkeeper, command that the door be opened, for we are travellers that will tarry no longer than to bait our horses and away, for we ride post-haste.'

'Doth it seem to you, gentlemen,' said Don Quixote, 'that I look like an Innkeeper?'

'I know not what thou lookest like,' answered the other, 'but well I know that thou speakest madly in calling this Inn a Castle.'

'It is a Castle,' replied Don Quixote, 'and one of the best in this Province, and it hath people in it who have had a sceptre in hand and a Crown on their head.'

'They be some company of strolling players, then,' replied the man, laughing, 'for no others hold sceptres or wear crowns in such a paltry Inn as this is.'

'Thou knowest but little of the world,' answered Don Quixote, 'seeing thou art ignorant of the chances that are wont to happen in Knight Errantry.'

The man's companions wearied of this discourse, and turned again to knock with great fury at the door, and this time they not only waked the Innkeeper but also all the guests, and the former arose to demand their pleasure.

In the meantime it happened that one of the horses on which they rode came sniffing round Rozinante, who stood melancholy and sad, with his ears down, bearing up his outstretched Master. But being after all an animal of a friendly disposition to his own kind, he could not refrain from turning round to sniff at him who came towards him.

Scarce had he moved one step, when Don Quixote's two feet, which were close together, slipped, and, sliding from the saddle, the Knight would have fallen to the ground had he not remained hanging by the arm. This caused him so much pain that he felt that his wrist was being cut off or his arm torn away. For he hung so near to the ground that he touched it with the tips of his toes; and this increased his misery, for, feeling the little that was wanted to set his feet wholly on the ground, he struggled all he could to reach it, deceived by the hope that he could indeed touch it if he only stretched himself a little further.

THE DISPUTED POMMEL

CHAPTER XXVIII

Wherein is continued the wonderful Adventures
at the Inn

WHILE Don Quixote hung suspended between heaven
and earth, his outcries were so horrible that the Innkeeper ran to the door, and opened it hastily and in great
fright, to see who it was that roared so loud.

Maritornes, whom the cries had also awakened, guess-
ing what it was, ran to the hay-loft, and, unseen by any
one, loosed the halter that held up Don Quixote, and he
fell at once to the ground in the sight of the Innkeeper
and the four travellers, who, coming up to him, asked
him what ailed him.

He, without any answer slipped the halter from his

wrist, and, rising to his feet, leaped on Rozinante, braced on his shield, couched his lance, and, wheeling round the field, rode back at a hard-gallop, crying out: 'Whosoever shall dare to say that I have been with just title enchanted, if my Lady, the Princess Micomicona, will give me leave to do it, I say that he lies, and I challenge him to single combat.'

The travellers were amazed at his words, but the Host told them that they must not mind him, for he was out of his wits.

When Don Quixote saw that none of the four travellers made any account of him or answered his challenge, he was ready to burst with wrath and fury; and could he have found that a Knight Errant might lawfully accept and undertake another enterprise, having plighted his word and faith not to attempt any until he had finished that which he had first promised, he would have fallen upon them all, and made them give him an answer in spite of themselves.

Those in the Inn were now fully aroused, and had come with the Innkeeper to see the new arrivals. Whilst they were talking to the four travellers, in the big room where they had supped, they heard a noise outside, the cause of which was that some dishonest guests, who had stayed there that night, seeing all the people busy to know the cause of the four horsemen coming, had thought to escape scot free without paying their reckoning. But the Innkeeper, who attended his own affairs with more diligence than other men's, stopped them going out and demanded his money, upbraiding their dishonest conduct with such words, that they returned him an answer with their fists; and this they did so roundly that the poor Innkeeper was compelled to cry for help.

His wife and his daughter, seeing Don Quixote standing by, cried out to him: 'Help, Sir Knight! help my poor father, whom two wicked men are thrashing like a bundle of corn.'

To this Don Quixote answered leisurely and with great gravity: 'Beautiful damsel, your prayer cannot at the present time be granted, for I am not permitted to engage in any new adventure until I have finished the one I have promised to carry through. And all that I can now do in your service is what I now say to you. Run unto your father and bid him continue and maintain his battle manfully until I demand leave of the Princess Micomicona to help him out of his distress. For if she will give me leave, you may make sure that he will be delivered.'

'As I am a sinner,' cried Maritornes, who was standing by, 'before you get that leave you speak of my Master will be in the other world.'

'Permit me but to get the leave I speak of,' replied Don Quixote, 'and it matters not whether he be in the other world or no. For I would bring him back again in spite of the other world itself, or at least, I will take such a revenge on those that sent him there that you shall be well content.'

Without saying more he went in and fell on his knees before Dorothea, demanding her in knightly and courtly phrases that she would give him leave to go and aid the

Constable of the Castle who was then plunged in deep distress.

The Princess granted him leave very willingly, and instantly buckling on his shield, and laying hands on his sword, he ran to the Inn door where the two guests were still fighting with the Innkeeper. But as soon as he arrived he stopped and stood still, although Maritornes and the Hostess asked him twice or thrice the cause of his delay in assisting their master and husband.

'I delay,' said Don Quixote, 'because it is not permitted me to lay hands to my sword against Squire-like men who are not dubbed Knights. But call me here my Squire Sancho, for this defence and revenge belong to him as his duty.'

All this took place outside the Inn door, where fists and blows were given and taken much to the Innkeeper's cost, and to the rage and grief of Maritornes and the Hostess and her daughter, who were like to run mad on seeing Don Quixote's cowardice and the mischief their master, husband, and father was enduring.

However, though the laws of Knighthood hindered Don Quixote from fighting, he soon persuaded the guests, by his wise reproofs of their conduct, to leave the Innkeeper alone, and pay him what was owing by them; and all would have been at peace in the Inn if another traveller had not arrived there at this moment. This was none other than the Barber from whom Don Quixote took away the helmet of Mambrino, and Sancho Panza the harness or furniture of the ass, whereof he made an exchange of his own. And while the Barber was leading his beast to the stable, he caught sight of Sancho Panza mending some part of the pack-saddle, or pannel, as it was called.

As soon as he had eyed him he knew him, and at once set upon Sancho, saying: 'Ah, Sir thief, here I have you! Give up my basin and my pannel, with all the trappings you stole from me.'

Sancho, finding himself attacked so suddenly, laying fast hold of the pannel with one hand, with the other gave the Barber such a buffet that he bathed his teeth in blood. But for all that the Barber held fast his grip of the pannel, and cried out so loud that all within the house came to the noise and scuffle.

'Help, here, in the name of the King and justice,' shouted the Barber. 'For this thief and robber by the highways goeth about to kill me because I seek to get back my own goods.'

'Thou liest,' cried Sancho, 'for I am not a robber of the highways. And my Lord Don Quixote won these spoils in a fair battle.'

By this time Don Quixote himself had come to the spot, not a little proud to see how his Squire defended himself and attacked his enemy, and he took him from that moment to be a man of valour, and resolved in his own mind to dub him Knight on the first occasion that should offer, because he thought that the order of Knighthood would be well bestowed on him.

'Sirs,' said the puzzled and angry Barber, 'this pannel is as certainly mine, and I know it as well as if I had bred it, and there is my ass in the stable who will not let me

lie; so do but try it on him, and if it fit him not to a hair,
I am willing to be called infamous. And I can say more,
that on the very day on which they took my pannel from
me, they robbed me likewise of a new brazen basin
which had never been used, and cost me a crown.'

Here Don Quixote could no longer contain himself
from speaking, and, thrusting himself between the two,
to part them asunder, he caused the pannel to be placed
publicly upon the ground until the dispute should be
decided, and said: 'To the end that you may understand
the clear mistake which this good Squire labours under,
see how he calls that a basin, which was, and is, and always shall be, the helmet of Mambrino, which I took
from him by force in fair battle, and made myself lord
thereof in a lawful and warlike manner. In regard to
the pannel I meddle not; but I can say that my Squire
Sancho asked leave of me to take away the trappings of
this vanquished coward's horse, that he might adorn his
own withal. I gave him leave to do it, and he took them.
As for these being turned from a horse's furniture to an
ass's pannel, I can give no other reason than the common
one in affairs of Knighthood, that this is done by enchantment. And to confirm the truth of all I say, run,
friend Sancho, speedily, and bring me out the helmet
which this good fellow declares to be a basin.'

'By my faith, Sir,' said Sancho, 'if we have no better
proof of our story than what you say, the helmet of Mambrino is as arrant a basin as this fellow's trappings are a
pack-saddle.'

'Do what I command,' replied Don Quixote, 'for I cannot believe that all things in this Castle are governed by enchantment.'

Sancho went for the basin and brought it, and as soon as Don Quixote saw it, he took it in his hands and said: 'See, Sirs, with what face can this impudent Squire declare that this is a basin, and not the helmet that I have mentioned. I swear to you by the order of Knighthood which I profess, that this is the very same helmet which I won from him, without having added or taken anything from it.'

'There is no doubt of that,' said Sancho, 'for, since the time my Lord won it until now, he never fought but one battle with it, when he delivered the unlucky chained men. And but for this basin, I mean helmet, he had not escaped so free as he did, so thick a shower of stones rained all the time of that battle.'

DON QUIXOTE
ARRESTED

CHAPTER XXIX

Wherein is finally decided the Dispute about
Mambrino's Helmet and the Pannel

'GOOD Sirs,' cried the Barber, 'what do you think of those who will contend that this is not a basin but a helmet?'

'He that shall say the contrary,' said Don Quixote. 'I will make him know that he lies, if he be a Knight; and if he be but a Squire, that he lies and lies again a thousand times.'

The Barber Nicholas, Don Quixote's friend, who was then with the rest, had a mind to carry the jest further, and make them all laugh, so, speaking to the other Barber, he said: 'Sir Barber, or whoever you are, know that I am also of your profession, and have held a certificate for more than twenty years, and I know all the instruments of a Barber's art well. Moreover, in my youth I was a soldier, and I know what a helmet is like, and a morion, and a casque, and other kinds of soldier's arms. And therefore I say, always subject to better opinion, that this good piece which is laid here before us, and which this good Knight holds in his hand, not only is not a Barber's basin, but is as far from being one as white is from black. It is a helmet, though, as I think, not a complete helmet.'

'No, truly,' said Don Quixote, 'for it wants the half, namely the lower part and the visor.'

'That is true,' said the Curate, who understood his friend's intention. And Cardenio, Fernando, and his companions fell in with this design.

'Lord a' mercy!' cried the poor Barber, half beside himself. 'Is it possible that so many honourable men should say that this is no basin but a helmet? It is a thing to strike with amazement a whole University, be they never so wise. Enough; if this basin is a helmet, then must the pack-saddle be a horse's trappings.'

'To me it looks like a pack-saddle,' said Don Quixote, 'but I have already said I do not meddle with that matter.'

'Whether it be a pannel or not,' said the Curate, 'it is but for Don Quixote to say, for in these matters of Knighthood, all these gentlemen and myself bow to his knowledge.'

'Sirs,' said Don Quixote, 'so many and strange are the things that have befallen me in this Castle these two times I have lodged here, that it would be rash in me to pronounce a judgment in the matter. To those who say this is a basin and no helmet I have made my answer, but whether this be a pannel or the furniture of a horse I will leave it to others to decide.'

To those who knew Don Quixote's madness this was a matter of much laughter and good sport, but to the four travellers who had just arrived that morning, and who were officers of justice, and soldiers of the Holy Brotherhood, it seemed the greatest folly in the world.

But he that was most of all beside himself with wrath was the Barber, whose basin they had transformed before his face into the helmet of Mambrino, and whose pannel, he felt sure, would now be turned into the rich furniture and equipage of a great horse.

Those who were in the secret laughed heartily to see Don Fernando go up and down taking the opinion of this man and that, whispering in their ear that they might give their verdict to him in secret.

And after he had gone round to all those who knew Don Quixote, he said to the Barber in a loud voice: 'The truth is, good fellow, that I grow weary of asking so many opinions, for I no sooner ask what I want to know than they answer me that it is mere madness to say that this is the pannel of an ass, but rather is it the furniture of a horse, yes and of a chief horse of service.'

'May I never go to heaven,' said the poor distracted Barber, 'if you be not all deceived! It is a pannel and no horse's trappings. But the law takes it from me, and so farewell to it.'

The Barber's simplicity caused no less laughter than the follies of Don Quixote, who said: 'There is now no more to be done than for every one to take his own.'

But at that moment one of the four officers of justice, who had listened to the dispute, full of anger to hear such nonsense seriously spoken, cried out: 'If this be not a planned jest, I cannot understand why men of such intelligence as all these seem to be, should dare to say that this is not a basin nor this a pannel. For indeed it is as very a pannel as my father is my father, and he that hath said or will say anything else must be drunk.'

'Thou liest like a clownish knave,' said Don Quixote. And lifting up his lance, which he always held in his hand, he aimed such a blow at the trooper's plate that, if he had not avoided it, it would have thrown him to the ground.

The lance was broken into splinters by the fall of the blow, and the other troopers, seeing their comrade so misused, cried out for help in the name of the Holy Brotherhood. The Innkeeper, whose duty it was to help all officers of justice, ran for his sword, and stood by to help them. The Barber laid hold of his pannel, and Sancho Panza did the same. Don Quixote set hand to his sword and attacked the troopers, and Cardenio and Don Fernando took his part. The Curate cried out, the Hostess shrieked, the daughter screamed, Maritornes howled, while Dorothea and Lucinda stood frightened and amazed. The Barber battered Sancho, and Sancho pounded him back again, while Don Fernando got one of the troopers at his feet, and belaboured him soundly.

The Innkeeper cried aloud for help for the Holy Brotherhood, and all the Inn seemed full of wails, cries,
screeches, confusion, fears, terrors, disasters, slashes, buffets, cudgellings, kicks, and the shedding of blood.

In the midst of this chaos, Don Quixote began to imagine that he was plunged up to the ears in the battle
of the King Agramante, and he cried aloud in a voice
that thundered through the Inn, 'Hold all your hands,
put up your swords, and keep the peace, if you wish to
continue alive.'

That great and monstrous voice made them all stand
still; on which he continued: 'Did I not tell you, Sirs,
that this Castle was enchanted, and that some legion of
magicians did inhabit it. Note how the discord of King
Agramante's Camp is among us, so that we all of us fight,
and none know for what. Come, therefore, Master Curate, and make you peace and atonement between us,
for I swear that it is a great wrong and pity that so many
noblemen as we are here should be slain for so slight
causes.'

The Barber was well content that this should be so,
by reason that both his beard and his pannel had been
torn to pieces, and Sancho was at once obedient to his
Master's voice, as became a dutiful servant. As for the
troopers, when they learned Don Fernando's rank and
position, they were quieted, but they retired from the
brawl grumbling, and by no means satisfied with the turn
things had taken.

Now it happened that one of these officers—the very

one who was so buffeted by Don Fernando—had with him a warrant to take into custody one Don Quixote, who was charged with setting free certain galley slaves. As soon as he remembered this, he must needs try whether the description of Don Quixote tallied with the person before him.

He took from his bosom a scroll of parchment, and reading it very leisurely, for he was no great scholar, at every other word he stared at Don Quixote, and compared the marks of his warrant with those in the Knight's face, and found that without doubt he was the man that was wanted.

No sooner had he made up his mind about this than, holding the warrant in his left hand, he laid hold of Don Quixote's collar with his right so strongly that he could hardly breathe, and cried aloud: 'Aid for the Holy Brotherhood. And that you may see that I am in good earnest, read that warrant, wherein you shall find that this robber of the highways is to be taken into custody.'

The Curate took the warrant, and saw that what the trooper said was true, and that the marks described Don Quixote very nearly.

As for the Knight, when he found himself abused by so base a rascal—as he considered him—his anger was roused to its height, and he caught the trooper by the throat with both hands, in such a way that if he had not been speedily rescued by his companions, he would have given up his life there and then, before Don Quixote would have released his hold.

The Innkeeper was forced to assist his fellow-officer, and his wife, seeing her husband engaged anew in battle, raised a fresh cry, which was caught up by her daughter and Maritornes, who called for help from all the company.

Sancho, seeing all that passed, called out: 'By my faith, all that my Master hath said of the enchantments of this Castle is true, for it is not possible for a man to live quietly in it for an hour together.'

Don Fernando soon parted the trooper and Don Quixote, but the officers did not cease to demand their prisoner, and called on the others to help them to bind him and deliver him up to their pleasure, for so the service of the King and the Holy Brotherhood required, in whose name they demanded help in arresting this robber and brigand of the public paths and highways.

Don Quixote laughed to hear them speak so idly, and said with great calmness: 'Come hither, filthy and base-born crew. Dare you call the loosing of the enchained, the freeing of prisoners, the assisting of the wretched, the raising of such as are fallen, the giving to those in want—dare you, I say, call these things robbing on the highway? O infamous brood, how little do you know of the virtue which lies in Knight Errantry? We give you to understand the sin and error in which you lie, in not adoring the very shadow, much more the actual presence of a Knight Errant. Come hither, I say, and tell me who was the blockhead who signed a warrant of arrest against such a Knight as I am? Who was he, that knows not that

Knights Errant are free from all tribunals; their sword is their law, their valour their court, and their own will and pleasure their statutes? I say again, What madman was he that knows not the privileges that belong to a Knight Errant, from the day he is dubbed a Knight and devotes himself to a Knightly calling? What Knight Errant did ever pay tax or custom? What tailor ever had of him money for a suit of clothes? What Constable ever lodged him in his Castle, and made him pay his shot? What King hath not placed him at his own table? And, finally, what Knight Errant was there ever, is, or shall be in the world, who hath not the courage himself alone to give four hundred cudgellings to four hundred officers if they stand in his way?'

Whilst Don Quixote raved in this way, the Curate was trying to persuade the troopers that Don Quixote was out of his wits, and that even if they did arrest him they would have to release him afterwards, as he was a madman.

'Indeed,' said the Curate, 'you must not take him, nor do I believe that he will let himself be taken.'

The officers were with difficulty persuaded to this view, but they had seen enough of Don Quixote to convince them of his madness, and in the end they agreed that it was better the Curate should endeavour, as he proposed, to take him to his home, than that they should arrest him at the risk of their lives.

The dispute between Sancho and the Barber was now easily settled, for there was very little left of the pannel

for Sancho to keep; and the Curate, without Don Quixote knowing anything of it, gave the Barber eight *reals*
for the price of his basin, so that they should hear nothing further of the dispute of Mambrino's helmet.

THE MANNER OF DON QUIXOTE'S RETURN HOME

CHAPTER XXX

In which is finished the notable Adventures
of our good Knight

THE Curate and Don Fernando now took the Innkeeper
aside and settled all his claims against Don Quixote, for
he had sworn that neither Rozinante nor Sancho's Ass
should stir from the Inn until he was paid to the last
farthing. As for Don Quixote, as soon as he found himself free from all the quarrels by which he had been sur-
rounded, he held it high time to begin his voyage and
bring to an end the great adventure unto which he was
called and chosen.

Therefore, having made up his mind to depart, he
went and cast himself upon his knees before Dorothea

and said: 'I cannot but think, high and worthy Lady, that our abode in this Castle is nothing profitable, and may turn out to our disadvantage. For who knows but that your enemy the Giant hath learned by spies or other secret means how I intend to come and destroy him, and he may by now have fortified himself in some impregnable Castle or Fortress, against the strength of which even the force of mine invincible arm will be of little use. Therefore, dear Lady, let us by our diligence hinder his plans, and let us depart to the place where fortune calls us.'

Don Quixote said no more but awaited the answer of the beautiful Princess, who, with a lordly air and in a style not unworthy of Don Quixote himself, replied as follows: 'I thank you, Sir Knight, for the desire you show to assist me in this my great need, and I trust your desires and mine may suceced, that I may show you that there are some thankful women on earth. As for my departure, let it be as you wish, for I have no other will than that which is yours. Therefore dispose of me at your own pleasure, for she that hath once given the defence of her person unto you, and hath put into your hand the recovery of her estate, ought not to seek to do any other thing but that which your wisdom shall suggest.'

'Let our departure, then,' said Don Quixote, 'be immediate. Saddle me Rozinante, Sancho, and get ready your Ass and the Queen's palfrey, and let us take leave of the Constable and these other lords and depart instantly.'

Sancho, who was present at all this, stood wagging his head from side to side, and said: 'O my Lord, my Lord, how much more knavery is there in the little village than is talked of!'

'What can be noised abroad in any village or in any of the cities of the world to my discredit, villain?' asked his Master angrily.

'If you are angry,' said Sancho, 'I will hold my tongue and omit to say that which by the duty of a good Squire, and an honest servant, I am bound to tell you.'

'Say what thou wilt,' said Don Quixote, and he waited to hear what his Squire had to say.

'What I mean,' continued Sancho, 'and what I hold for most sure and certain is, that this Lady, who calls herself Queen of the great Kingdom of Micomicona, is no more a Queen than my mother. For if she were what she says, she would not at every corner be billing and cooing with one that is in this good company.'

Dorothea blushed at Sancho's words, for it was true indeed that her lover Don Fernando had sometimes on the sly gathered from her lips the reward of his affections. She was neither able nor willing to answer Sancho a word, but let him go on with his speech, which he did as follows:—

'This I say, good my Lord, to this end, that if after we have travelled highways and byways and endured bad nights and worse days, he that is in this Inn,' and Sancho looked knowingly at Don Fernando, 'shall marry our Princess and get the fruits of your labours, there is no need to hasten, methinks, to saddle Rozinante or harness Dapple, or make ready the palfrey seeing it would be better that we stayed still and looked after our dinner.'

You may imagine how great was the fury that inflamed Don Quixote when he heard his Squire speak so rudely. It was so great that, with a shaking voice, a faltering tongue, and the fire sparking out of his eyes, he said: 'O villainous peasant, rash, unmannerly, ignorant, rude, foul-mouthed backbiter and slanderer! Darest thou utter such words in my presence and in that of these noble Ladies? Hast thou dared to entertain such rash and stupid fancies in thy muddled imagination? Out of my sight, monster of nature, storehouse of untruth, armoury of falsehood, sink of roguery, inventor of villainy, publisher of ravings, enemy of the respect due to Royal persons. Away, villain, and never more appear before me on pain of my wrath.'

So saying, he bent his brows and glared around on every side as he struck a mighty blow upon the ground with his right foot. And at these words and furious gestures, poor Sancho was so greatly frightened, that he could have wished in that instant that the earth opening under his feet would swallow him up.

But the witty Dorothea, who now understood Don Quixote's humour perfectly, to appease his anger spoke to him thus: 'Be not offended, good Sir Knight of the Rueful Countenance, at the idle words your good Squire hath spoken. For perhaps he hath not said them without some ground, and we cannot suspect from a man of his good understanding that he would knowingly slander or accuse any one falsely. And therefore we must believe that without doubt, as you have yourself said, Sir Knight, in this Castle all things are subject to enchantment, and it might well happen that Sancho may have been deceived by some wicked illusion.'

'I vow,' cried Don Quixote, 'that your Highness has hit the truth, and that some evil vision appeared to this sinner, my man Sancho, that made him see things that he could not have seen unless by enchantment. For I also know very well, that the great goodness and simplicity of the poor wretch is such, that he knows not how to invent a lie on anybody living.'

'It is even so,' said Don Fernando; 'and therefore, good Sir Don Quixote, you must pardon him and take him once more to the bosom of your grace.'

Don Quixote answered that he did willingly pardon him; and Sancho, kneeling down on his knees, humbly asked his Lord's hand, which he gave to him. And after he had permitted him to kiss it, he gave him his blessing, saying: 'Now thou shalt finally know, Sancho, that which I have told thee many times, how that all things in this Castle come about by means of enchantment.'

And this Sancho was ready to believe of everything except the tossing they had given him in the blanket, for he well knew that he had been tossed by persons of flesh and blood and bone, and not by visionary and unreal phantoms and shadows, as his Master was always telling him.

Two days passed, when it seemed to all the noble company at the Inn that it was time to depart, and they considered how, without putting Dorothea and Don Fernando to the pain of turning back with Don Quixote to his village, the Curate and the Barber could carry him home as they desired, and leave him cured of his folly in his own home.

This was the plan they decided on. They made a bargain with a wagoner, who chanced to pass by that way with a team of oxen, to carry him in the following manner:—

They made a thing like a cage of timber, so big that Don Quixote might sit or lie in it at his ease, and presently Don Fernando, Cardenio, their companions, and the Innkeeper did all, by Master Curate's directions, cover their faces and disguise themselves as well as they could, so that they might seem to Don Quixote to be different persons to any he had seen in the Castle. This being done, they entered silently into the place where he slept, reposing after his recent battles. They went up to him as he was sleeping peacefully, not fearing any such accident, and, laying hold of him forcibly, they tied his hands and feet very strongly, so that when he started out of his sleep he could not move, nor do anything else but stare and wonder at the strange faces that he saw before him.

And immediately he fell into the idea, which his wild imagination had at once suggested to him, that all these strange figures were spirits and phantoms of that enchanted Castle, and he believed that he himself was without doubt enchanted, seeing that he could neither move nor defend himself.

All happened as the Curate who plotted the jest expected; and after they had brought him to the cage, they shut him within, and afterwards nailed the bars thereof so well that they could not easily be broken. Sancho all this time looked on in wonder to see what would happen to his Master.

Then the phantoms mounted him upon their shoulders, and as he was carried out of his chamber door the Barber called out in as terrible a voice as he could muster: 'O Knight of the Rueful Countenance, be not grieved at thine imprisonment, for so it must be that thine adventures be more speedily ended. And thou, O most noble and obedient Squire that ever had sword at girdle, beard on a face, or dent in a nose, let it not dismay thee to see carried away thus the flower of all Knighthood. For I assure thee that all thy wages shall be paid to thee, if thou wilt follow in the steps of this valorous and enchanted Knight. And as I am not allowed to say more, farewell!'

Don Quixote listened attentively to all this prophecy, and said: 'O thou, whatsoever thou beest, I desire thee to request in my name that I may not perish in this prison before my work is ended. And as concerns my Squire Sancho Panza, I trust in his goodness that he will not abandon me in good or bad fortune. For, though it should fall out through his or my hard lot that I shall not be able to bestow on him an Island, as I have promised, his wages cannot be lost to him, for in my Will, which is made already, I have set down what he is to have for his many good services.'

Sancho Panza bowed his head with great reverence when he heard this, and kissed both his Master's hands, which were bound tightly together. Then the phantoms lifted up the cage and hoisted it on to the wagon that was drawn by the team of oxen.

After bidding farewell to all their friends, the procession started. First went the cart guided by the carter, then the troopers, then followed Sancho upon his Ass leading Rozinante by the bridle, and last of all the Curate and the Barber, riding their mighty mules, with masks on their faces.

Don Quixote sat with his hands tied and his legs stretched out, leaning against a bar of the cage, with such a silence and such patience that he seemed rather to be a statue than a man. And thus at an Alderman-like pace, such as suited the slow steps of the heavy oxen, they journeyed home.

At the end of two days they arrived at Don Quixote's village, into which they entered about noon. This was on a Sunday, when all the people were in the marketplace, through the midst of which Don Quixote's cart passed. All drew near to see what was in it, and when they knew their neighbour they were greatly astounded. A little boy ran home before, to tell the old woman and the Niece that their Lord and Uncle was returned. It would have moved one to pity to have heard the cries and lamentations the two good women made, and the curses they poured out against all Books of Knighthood, when they saw Don Quixote enter the gates of his own house again in so strange a carriage.

Sancho Panza's wife, when she heard of his return, ran forward to meet her husband, and the first question she asked was whether the Ass were in health or no.

Sancho answered that he was come in better health than his master.

'Tell me, then,' cried his wife, 'what profit hast thou reaped by this Squireship? What petticoat hast thou brought me home? What shoes for the little boys?'

'I bring none of these things, good wife,' replied Sancho, 'though I bring things better thought of and of greater moment.'

'I am glad of that,' said his wife, 'for I should like to see them, to the end that my heart may be cheered, which hath been swollen and sorrowful for so long, all the time of thine absence.'

'Thou shalt see them at home,' said Sancho, 'therefore rest satisfied. For when we travel once again to seek adventures, thou shalt see me shortly afterwards an Earl or Governor of an Island, one of the best in the world.'

'I pray that it may be so,' replied his wife; 'but what means that Island, for I understand not the word?'

'Honey is not made for the ass's mouth,' said Sancho, 'but thou shalt know all in good time. Do not busy thyself, Joan, to know all things in a sudden. It is enough that I will tell thee all the truth, and therefore close thy mouth. I will only say this much unto thee as yet, that there is nothing in the world so pleasant as for an honest man to be the Squire of a Knight that seeks adventures.'

.   .   .   .   .   .

Now, if I were to tell you that Don Quixote got quite well and lived quietly at home after all these adventures, and never went abroad again, I should tell you what is not true. For some day, and I hope at no great distance of time, you may read what the great Cervantes has written, not only of the adventures of which I have told you the story, but of the second part of Don Quixote's adventures, some of which are even more wonderful than the first. There you will learn how Sancho Panza became at last Governor of an Island for a short space, and may read of the great wisdom and shrewdness with which he ruled.

All these good things will be yours to read some day, as they have been mine and are every one's. For, like all the really great stories of the world, this of Don Quixote belongs to no nation or people, but is the property of each and all of us, given us freely to enjoy it how and where we will. And from the humour and wisdom of such books we may become brighter and better ourselves. So that when I wish that you may be able to love and honour all such books, and to read this one as Cervantes wrote it, and with the care it deserves to be read, it is the best wish I can give you. And, indeed, to wish you the gift of understanding it, is the same thing as wishing you a happy life.